KV-380-385

Hellfire

Hellfire's outlaw gang raided a train bound for Calamity and carrying $50,000. But Marshal Lincoln Hawk thwarted their plans and, in the chaos, eighteen innocent townsfolk were killed and the money went missing.

Sixteen years later, a vengeful Hellfire escapes from prison and goes in search of the missing money. But in the now abandoned Calamity, Marshal Hawk has appointed himself as Hellfire's judge, jury and executioner and is waiting for him.

Can either of them discover what happened to the money? And who is the ghostly figure haunting the station? Only one thing is certain – when the gunsmoke clears just one man will be left standing.

By the same author

Ambush in Dust Creek
Silver Gulch Feud
Blood Gold
Golden Sundown
Clearwater Justice

ROSSINGTON
868205
S/de
—TRL

R

16 APR 2009

18 OCT 2009

31 MAR 2014

2 2 MAY 2014

2 0 OCT 2006

ASKERN
Tel: 700324
7/08

25 JUN 2010

27 AUG 2011

29 MAY 2015

Thorne
01405 746969

12 AUG 2016

11 AUG 2008   06/12

13 AUG 2008   2 0 AUG 2012

18 SEP 2012

18 OCT 2008

5 SEP 2016

16 FEB 2017

22 APR 2017

1 - NOV 2012

CANTLEY
Tel:535614

3/13

02 JUL 2018

25 JUL 2018

RoS

13 APR 2019

Doncaster
Metropolitan Borough Council

DONCASTER LIBRARY AND INFORMATION SERVICES

Please return/renew this item by the last date shown.
Thank you for using your library.

DONCASTER LIBRARY SERVICE

30122 03084026 4

Hellfire

Scott Connor

A Black Horse Western

ROBERT HALE · LONDON

© Scott Connor 2006
First published in Great Britain 2006

ISBN-10: 0-7090-7960-5
ISBN-13: 978-0-7090-7960-6

Robert Hale Limited
Clerkenwell House
Clerkenwell Green
London EC1R 0HT

The right of Scott Connor to be identified as
author of this work has been asserted by him
in accordance with the Copyright, Designs and
Patents Act 1988.

DONCASTER LIBRARY AND INFORMATION SERVICE	
30122030840264	
Bertrams	23.03.06
W	£10.99

Typeset by
Derek Doyle & Associates, Shaw Heath.
Printed and bound in Great Britain by
Antony Rowe Limited, Wiltshire.

CHAPTER 1

The fire was already raging out of control. Only minutes after Sheriff McCarthy had heard the prisoners' first cries of alarm the flames had became an inferno and converted the small jailhouse into a hellish place of death.

Earlier that day he had received a consignment of prisoners, all of them lifers, who were being transferred to a new prison. But no matter how worthless these men were, the lawman reckoned that their panicked cries would fuel his nightmares for years.

Deputy Lynch joined him, still shrugging into his clothes, and the two lawmen stared at the building. But as the flames erupted before them, ensuring that neither man could get within twenty feet of the building, the sheriff pulled his deputy back.

'It's hopeless,' he shouted.

'It is,' Lynch shouted back, 'but we got to do something.'

'There's nothing we can do but pray for their

souls and make sure the fire doesn't spread beyond the compound.'

In that they were lucky, the jailhouse was on the edge of Lester Forks and at least fifty yards beyond the nearest building.

'Any idea how it started?' Lynch asked.

With an arm up to shield his face from the heat, McCarthy shrugged.

'No idea. Guess one of the prisoners tried a wild scheme to escape and it went wrong.'

'Or it didn't and this is to cover up his escape.'

McCarthy nodded, already dreading the search through the wreckage for bodies when the fire died down.

'Guess we should . . .'

McCarthy flinched as the jailhouse door rattled then flew open. A prisoner hurtled through. His clothes were ablaze and flames trailed behind him. With frantic gestures, he tugged at his jacket and threw it to the ground, but smoke still plumed from his shirt and he dropped, then rolled in the dirt.

The two lawmen broke into a run and joined him. McCarthy grabbed his shoulders while Lynch kicked dirt over him.

'Obliged,' the prisoner shouted, still squirming within his smouldering clothing.

'Any more in there alive?' McCarthy asked, while Lynch stamped on the man's discarded jacket.

'There is,' a voice intoned from behind him.

McCarthy started to turn, but at that moment the man on the ground took advantage of the

6

distraction to leap up. His hand closed on McCarthy's holster then tore out his gun. Within a moment McCarthy found that the man had his own gun on him. He could do nothing but raise his hands, but that didn't concern him as much as the steady footfalls from behind.

He turned. Silhouetted against the burning jailhouse stood a man, standing with legs astride and smoke rising from his clothes. Behind him, two other prisoners scampered out. One man smacked his jacket against the ground to extinguish the burning cloth while the other man slapped his arms and legs as if he were engaging in a wild dance. But the central man appeared oblivious to the smoke rising from his hat and clothes as he stared at McCarthy, his eyes twinkling.

'You set the jailhouse alight, didn't you?' McCarthy said.

'Sure did,' the man said, his voice light and unconcerned by the screaming still ripping out from the building behind him.

'And who are you?'

The man strode towards McCarthy, looking him up and down as stray tendrils of smoke spiralled away in his wake.

He had a large mark on his cheek, perhaps a birthmark, and eyes that burned with savage malevolence. He stomped to a halt and, with an almost casual gesture, flipped his smouldering hat to the ground.

'They call me Hellfire,' he said. 'And you're about to find out why.'

*

'What you want?' Harvey Baez asked.

Before him, the three men stood before the trading-post door, the early-evening breeze rippling their long coats. With slow, deliberate paces, they strode to the counter and lined up.

'Shelton Baez,' the lead man said through gritted teeth.

'And who wants . . .' Harvey gulped to loosen his tight throat as a cold fire flared the man's eyes. 'I'll go fetch him.'

He edged back a pace, then hurried into the storeroom and demanded that his uncle come quickly.

'Sort this out yourself,' Shelton murmured then waved in a dismissive manner at him while continuing to count his stock.

'But I ain't seen these customers before.' Harvey pointed back into the main room. 'And they don't look like they want to buy anything, if you know what I mean.'

Shelton snapped up to stand straight and closed his eyes for a moment.

'What do they look like?'

'Three men, surly, long coats.'

'Any of them got a mark on his face?'

'Nope.'

Shelton sighed and placed a hand to his chest.

'Then go outside.'

'And do what?'

'Just go!' Shelton grunted, then brushed past

Harvey and into the store, his back straight and his gaze cold and distant.

Harvey edged towards the back door, but in the doorway he wavered, then shuffled back across the storeroom to peer around the door at the newcomers.

'You came quickly,' Shelton said.

'We don't waste time,' a gruff voice replied. 'Who you got?'

'His given name is Jeremiah Court, but he goes by the name of . . .' Shelton glanced over his shoulder towards the door, but Harvey had anticipated his move and darted his head back. 'They call him Hellfire.'

Giddiness reeled Harvey back against the wall. His guts rumbled and he had to gulp deeply to fight down the bile that burned his throat.

'Never heard of him,' the man grunted.

'He's spent the last sixteen years in prison, but three weeks ago they tried to transport him to a new prison. He escaped.'

The first twinge of a potential headache throbbed as Harvey shuffled closer to the door and peered through the gap between the door and the wall. He saw the man nod.

'We charge five hundred dollars.' The man leaned on the counter and raised his eyebrows. 'Can you afford that?'

'Keep Hellfire away from me, permanently, and I'll pay you one thousand.'

The man glanced over his shoulder, receiving nods from his colleagues then turned back.

'Then you just hired us. When you expecting this Hellfire?'

'Any day.' Shelton glanced at the door and shivered. 'Perhaps even tonight.'

Harvey wanted to hear more, but through the gap he saw two of the men spread out and wander around the post. The lead man glanced at the door. Harvey, although he guessed that he wouldn't be able to see him, darted back from the doorway, then left the storeroom through the back exit.

Outside, he sat on the old dug-out and looked west towards the railroad and the town of Stark Pass, the trading post's nearest settlement now that Calamity had been abandoned. The dying sun was dipping below the far mountains, bleeding deep red rays across the land and stretching long shadows away from every boulder.

'One thousand dollars,' he murmured to himself, 'one zero zero zero. Can't be that much money in the whole world.'

With a hand to his brow, Harvey watched the last sliver of sun fade away, trying to keep his mind from dwelling on the fear that these men's sudden arrival and Shelton's mention of Hellfire had instilled in him.

But then Shelton shouted some orders at him from inside. So, he stood and wandered round to the front of the post to care for the men's horses.

But to his side he saw movement. Harvey flinched, but when he turned, all was still. He squinted as he ran his gaze over the ridge that loomed over the trading post, but still saw nothing.

10

Then the movement came again and Harvey jerked his head round to confront it. A half-mile down the ridge, on the edge of a rocky outcrop, a solitary figure stood, the form standing out in sharp relief against the red sky.

With his eyes narrowed to slits, Harvey reckoned it was a slight person, perhaps a woman, a cape wrapped around her, the trailing ends fluttering behind her in the breeze.

He blinked hard to ensure the figure wasn't just a burst of sun-blindness, and when he reopened his eyes the figure had gone.

Harvey bit back his flash of disappointment then smiled.

'You're back,' he whispered to himself.

CHAPTER 2

Marshal Lincoln Hawk drew his horse to a halt. Hunched forward in the saddle, he stared into what was left of the town.

The moment he had heard that Hellfire had escaped he knew that he had to be the one who tracked him down. But with Hellfire covering his tracks, nobody had got a lead on him.

But Lincoln reckoned he knew where Hellfire would go, so he'd gone directly to Calamity, but his destination was as unrewarding as he'd feared.

The last decade hadn't been kind to the town. The mouldering remnants of what could have been a fine town were now a festering sore beside the railroad. The buildings that still stood were shells, hinting only at their former glory.

The boardwalks had rotted. The standing structures teetered. The signs that once proudly advertised the stores and saloons had faded and dangled from rusting nails.

None of the buildings' timber had been salvaged to build elsewhere; but then again, after what had happened here, Lincoln wasn't surprised.

Ahead of his deputies, Alvin Buckfast and Daniel Samuels, Lincoln rode through the dusty ghost town and stopped before the burnt-out remnants of the train station, the original heart of the town, and then its death.

Here Lincoln dismounted and paced to the edge of the platform. He bowed his head as he strode over the rotting timbers to stand beside the railroad. With his legs planted wide, he looked down the tracks, as if awaiting a train – just as he'd done sixteen years ago.

Alvin and Daniel lingered behind him, then they nudged each other and Alvin shuffled across the platform to join him.

'What happened here?' he asked.

Lincoln looked over Alvin's shoulder at the wrecked station, then down a road that should be bustling and prosperous, searching for the memories that rarely came these days while fighting back the memories that would never leave him.

'Hellfire happened,' he said.

Then he paced over the tracks to stand on the very same spot on which he and Marshal Billy Epstein had stood that day.

'You ain't doing that, Lincoln,' Billy had said to him, his sneering expression and steadfast refusal to listen to advice as fresh today in Lincoln's memory as it had been on that fine summer afternoon.

13

'We got no choice,' Lincoln said. He worked for the railroad then and had no right to order a town marshal around, but when that lawman was acting like an idiot, he thought it was time for someone with sense to take control.

Earlier that day an outlaw gang led by Jeremiah Court, also known as Hellfire, had ridden into town and raided the train when it'd pulled up at the station. Hellfire reckoned $50,000 was being transported on it, but when he didn't find the money he had held everyone who had been awaiting the train hostage, then given the railroad twelve hours to come up with the money.

Twelve hours passed after that ultimatum and although the money was piled in a cage behind the train Marshal Epstein had taken it upon himself to call Hellfire's bluff.

'We got every choice,' Billy said. 'We got him trapped in there and we can wait him out.'

'We can't. Give him the money, or give him a way out, but don't sit him out or innocent people are going to start dying.'

As the marshal shook his head, the acrid taint of burning assailed Lincoln's nostrils. He peered around the back of the train and saw tendrils of smoke spiralling up from the station roof. A flame flickered at one of the windows.

'Hellfire's torched the station,' Billy murmured. 'Why would he do that?'

'Because the twelve hours are up, as I've been telling you, and because burning the station down is precisely what he'd do.'

'And how would you know that?' Billy sneered.

'They call him Hellfire. There's got to be a reason.'

Billy rubbed his chin as he rocked from foot to foot. In that moment Lincoln decided that if all lawmen were as ineffectual as this one, he'd consider becoming one himself. But that was for another day, and now the station roof was alight and the shooting was starting.

While the marshal ordered his deputies to stay back and see what Hellfire did next, Lincoln hurried out from behind the train. Billy called him back, but he ignored him and continued running. He aimed to get square on to the station then run in from the side where there were no windows. Then he could try to get into the building and get the hostages out; but as he closed on the station three men burst out from the back of the building.

Two gawping members of the townsfolk were loitering on Calamity's main road and the outlaws instantly cut them down, then ran for their horses.

Lincoln glanced left and right. To his left, Hellfire's men were trying to escape. To his right, the station was ablaze.

Despite the draw of getting into the station, he ran towards the men. On the run, he tore an arc of gunfire into them, cutting one man off with a shot to the side, then slicing through the next two. These men stumbled on for a few paces, then flopped to the ground to lie face down.

Lincoln ran on, reloading as he darted his gaze at the station, then at the other outlaws who were venturing out on to the platform. One outlaw swirled round to face Lincoln and fired wildly, then hunkered down to take more careful aim, but Lincoln threw himself to the ground to lie on his belly. With his gun thrust out, he slammed the man to the ground with a high shot to the neck, then rolled again, coming to his feet, and set off again.

Now just twenty feet from the station, he saw two outlaws gain their horses, but then at last the marshal acted. With his deputies around him, he surged around the other side of the station and lay down a burst of gunfire that spooked the horses and kept the outlaws from making a run for it.

Then Lincoln saw Hellfire himself. He was scooting along the side of the station, keeping under the eaves, the flames shooting out from the windows and door around him, but a burst of gunfire from one of the marshal's deputies forced him to retreat.

Lincoln side-stepped behind the side of the station and waited, the heat from the fire inside already permeating the wall and warming his back. Long seconds passed, every heartbeat only helping to erode Lincoln's belief that waiting was the right thing to do, but Lincoln got his reward when Hellfire hurried out on his side of the station. And he had his back to him.

Lincoln stepped out behind Hellfire.

'Reach,' he ordered.

Hellfire turned at the hip, his gun arcing round to aim at Lincoln, but Lincoln blasted a single shot, snatching the gun from his hand. And then he was on him.

Hellfire sneered at Lincoln, his hands half-raised.

'Go on,' he murmured without a trace of fear in his eyes. 'Shoot.'

'Not doing that,' Lincoln said. 'I reckon the rest of your men will fight until nobody comes out of there alive, but one word from you and they'll give up.'

Hellfire licked his lips. 'And the deal if I help you?'

'I ain't no lawman. I can't offer no deal, but I reckon it'll sound better for you if you give yourself up.'

Hellfire glanced at the burning station, then shrugged.

'No deal.'

Lincoln winced. Then, as he saw nothing in Hellfire's eyes to suggest he'd ever co-operate, he dragged him away from the burning station to get him into the custody of the marshal's deputies.

As he edged back across the platform the shooting continued in sporadic bursts from the other side of the station. But even some distance from the fighting Lincoln could see that Marshal Epstein had placed his men in all the wrong places. They weren't giving Hellfire's men any problems, but the fire was. It had now taken hold of most of the station and if Lincoln and the ineffectual lawman didn't end this siege quickly, a lot of people were about to die.

Lincoln gained a tighter grip of Hellfire's shoulders and speeded his journey across the platform, but when he reached the train none of the marshal's deputies was there. So, he searched for a place to secure Hellfire while he rejoined the fighting. Then saw something that rocked him back on his heels – the cage and the $50,000 were no longer there.

Lincoln glanced around, then assumed that one of the deputies had found a safer place for the money. So he found a rope and quickly secured Hellfire, then hurried over to join the marshal, now turning his thoughts to how they could end this ambush with the hostages coming out alive.

But he was already too late.

And neither did anyone find the missing money. . . .

In the present, Lincoln shook himself, freeing his thoughts from those terrible events and turned to Alvin.

'I caught Hellfire, but his gang escaped. By then, the station was ablaze and we couldn't get in. They'd tied everyone up and eighteen people burned to death. It took some months, but we tracked down every last one of his gang, but Hellfire never got the justice he deserved.'

Alvin winced. 'Why?'

'He claimed the fire broke out when his woman, Adele, accidentally knocked over an oil-lamp.' Lincoln paced over the tracks and back on to the platform. 'The only hostage to survive was Shelton

Baez, and he didn't see how the fire started.'

'But you knew Hellfire was lying?'

'Sure did.'

Lincoln continued walking across the platform. When he reached the edge he counted ten steps to a spot on the edge of the main road. He turned, measuring the distance to the station. This was where he'd held Hellfire at gunpoint. But he'd let him live to get real justice. And although that failure to receive justice was the one last spur he'd needed to become a lawman, he had never forgotten Hellfire.

Lincoln turned, dismissing that terrible day from his mind, and headed to his horse, his deputies trailing behind him.

'And afterwards,' Alvin said, 'they didn't rebuild the station?'

'Nobody had the guts to carry on after that big a tragedy. The station moved down the track and Stark Pass grew up, leaving Calamity to die.'

Alvin nodded, but behind them Daniel screeched a warning, then drew his gun and turned at the hip to aim his gun at the station.

Alvin and Lincoln both drew their guns and dashed back down the road to join him. The three men stood in a defensive circle, their guns drawn and aimed around the deserted ghost town.

'What you see?' Alvin asked from the corner of his mouth.

Daniel peered into the ruined station and narrowed his eyes.

'Somebody's moving around in there.'

Lincoln glanced at the wrecked skeleton of the building. The only movement came from a trapped rag flicking in the wind.

'Nobody's lived in Calamity for years.'

'Except for ghosts,' Alvin said. He smirked and put on a false, high voice. 'And maybe one of them might come out of the station and—'

Daniel shivered. 'Don't mock me. When that much death happens, the ghosts never leave.'

'Spare me your spooky tales,' Lincoln snapped and swung his gun back into his holster. 'I don't believe in that nonsense. I worry more about the living ghosts.'

CHAPTER 3

The man appeared to have blood splattered over his face, but Marshal Cooper noted that the bartender was trying not to stare.

'Whiskey,' the man grunted.

The bartender swung a whiskey-bottle on to the counter and sloshed a full glass, again taking the opportunity to glance at the man.

From his position at the end of the bar Cooper decided that the blood wasn't fresh. It was a blemish, perhaps an old burn, which covered most of his right cheek and spread out beneath the eye.

But then that eye twitched and the bartender lowered his head.

'See anything interesting?' The man ripped back his hat and thrust his face to the side, his cheek held high. 'Want to stare some more at my mark?'

'I'm sorry,' the bartender murmured. 'Have the first drink on me.'

The man snorted and hurled a handful of coins on to the bar.

'I ain't looking for your pity.' He turned and leaned back against the bar, then looked to the saloon door.

Cooper saw that, outside, at least a dozen men were lined up at the hitching rail. Most stayed mounted, leaving three men to clump on to the boardwalk and file in through the batwings. From under lowered hats these men glanced around the saloon, then, with a swaggering gait, headed to the bar.

Cooper swirled his whiskey as, from the corner of his eye, he watched the men stomp to a halt before the bar.

'Whiskeys for you three,' the bartender said, beaming. 'And if you like what you drink, maybe you'll enjoy a longer stay.'

The man with the blemish snorted and swung round to face the bartender.

'Quit the talk. I want Shelton Baez.'

'Shelton Baez,' the bartender intoned, scratching his forehead, then glanced down the bar at Cooper.

Cooper fingered his glass, then downed his whiskey and paced down the bar to face the newcomers. With his steady gaze he sized them up. He didn't like what he saw.

'We've never heard of him,' Cooper said.

The man gulped his whiskey, then swirled the dregs.

'He worked with another good-for-nothing runt, Lincoln Hawk, at the railroad office in Calamity.'

'Ain't been anything like that in Calamity

since . . .' Cooper rubbed his chin as he considered. '. . . fifteen years ago. Railroad office is here now, so you might try—'

'I ain't interested in asking them,' the man murmured, still not looking at Cooper. 'I *am* asking you.'

'Nope. Still don't know him.'

A flicked glance from the blemished man encouraged the other men to stand around Cooper. They raised their heels so that they could peer down at him. One man brushed imaginary dust from Cooper's shoulders, and the man who was out of Cooper's eye-line snorted a laugh at nothing in particular.

Cooper just folded his arms and kept his stance casual. But from his table in the corner Brock Crowthers was wandering to the bar, leaving his drinking-partner to scrape back his chair and watch him with interest.

'You looking for Shelton Baez, you say?' Brock said, swinging to a halt. He provided a gap-toothed smile, but received a firm glare in return.

'Yeah.'

Brock tapped his white-bristled chin, his brow furrowed with mock effort.

'Baez, Baez, Baez,' he mused. Brock licked his lips, then glanced at the whiskey-bottle on the bar and grinned hopefully. 'The name sounds mighty familiar, but I can't remember much when I'm right thirsty.'

The man reached down the bar to finger the whiskey-bottle, then scraped it along the bar to just

23

out of Brock's reach.

'Tell me where he is and you get the bottle.'

Unbidden, Brock's outstretched fingers drifted towards the bottle, before he snapped the hand into a fist and shook his head.

'Make it a full bottle and it's a deal.' Brock shrugged. 'It's a mighty long story.'

'You got yourself a deal.'

'Brock,' Cooper urged, but Brock's whoop of delight drowned him out.

'And who,' Brock said, grinning, 'wants him?'

The man licked his lips. When he spoke he uttered his single word with an exaggerated movement of the mouth.

'Hellfire.'

Cooper threw his hand to his holster, but the man who was standing behind him grabbed his arm, then yanked it half-way up his back.

In a skipped heartbeat Brock paled, but even as his mouth was falling open, the blemished man, Hellfire, lunged. He grabbed Brock's collar and dragged him up close, then cocked his head to the side, displaying his blemish as he looked down into Brock's eyes.

'I was . . . I was just dragging out a yarn to get me a drink,' Brock babbled. His scrawny neck bulged as he delivered a pronounced gulp. 'I don't know nothing about no—'

'You were, were you?' Hellfire drew his gun and thrust the barrel under Brock's chin.

'Hey,' Cooper said. 'Ain't no need for no threats. If Brock says he doesn't know where this

24

Shelton Baez is, he doesn't.'

With a mocking shake of the head, Hellfire admonished Cooper, then turned his firm gaze back on Brock.

'I ain't got time for you to tell me no long story.' Hellfire thrust the barrel deep into Brock's flesh, forcing him up on to tiptoes. 'So, tell me where I can find Shelton Baez.'

'Like you said, he worked for the railroad, but that was years ago,' Brock said, then flashed a desperate grin. 'Then he moved on. Last I heard he was running this trading post.'

'Where?'

'I . . . I don't know.'

'Try harder!' Hellfire widened his eyes.

'I don't know. I just don't.'

'Wrong answer.' Hellfire squeezed the trigger, blasting Brock's head up and away from him, his bloodied body dead before it hit the floor.

Cooper struggled but the man holding him wrapped his arm around his neck so tightly it closed his windpipe. As he fought for breath he could only watch in horror as the bartender ran for the door. But one of Hellfire's men ripped a bullet into his hip, which knocked him sideways a pace. Then he followed through with a second slug to the head that crashed the bartender through the window.

Before the shards of glass had clattered to the ground Brock's drinking-partner leapt to his feet. He hurled his hand to his gun. But as he dragged it from its holster Hellfire thundered a low slug

25

into his chest which slammed him back against the wall.

The man righted himself. With grim determination he returned a shot that whistled by Hellfire's arm. But Hellfire's men returned a hail of gunfire that wheeled him to the floor.

Repeated gunfire made the body twitch and dance as if it were still alive while Hellfire's men gibbered with delight. Only when they'd spent their bullets did they stop.

A shroud of gunsmoke hung in the air, the acrid taint making Cooper's eyes water, as Hellfire swung round and aimed his gun straight at Cooper's forehead.

'Now,' he muttered, 'where is Shelton Baez?'

Cooper gulped as he stared down the barrel of the gun. He glanced at each of the bodies lying in the saloon, then turned back to face Hellfire.

'You just got to believe me. I don't know nothing about him.'

Hellfire gestured and the man holding Cooper folded the lawman over the counter.

'Then listen to this.' Hellfire gestured to the man on his left, who grabbed Cooper's wrist and thrust his hand flat to the counter, then splayed the fingers. 'Talk to me. If I like what I hear, I leave. If I don't like what I hear, I do this.'

Hellfire placed the barrel of his gun over Cooper's smallest finger. Cooper tried to flinch away but the man holding his hand had a grip of iron. Cooper babbled, begging Hellfire not to do anything. Then Hellfire fired.

Hot fire ripped into Cooper's finger. He closed his eyes, his back rigid as he steeled himself for the pain, but when it didn't come with the intensity he expected he opened his eyes, hoping that maybe, just maybe, nothing had happened.

But then he saw the blackened stump of his finger and he swung his head to the side to vomit down the side of the bar.

'Now,' Hellfire said, slamming the barrel over Cooper's second finger, 'talk before I run out of bits to shoot off you.'

'You reckon you'll be able to keep this Hellfire away?' Harvey Baez asked.

The leader of Shelton's hired guns, Eli Payton, raised a foot on to the bottom rail of the corral fence and leaned on his knee.

'The likes of Hellfire don't worry me,' he said, then spat to the side.

The week since Eli, Garth and Jackson had arrived at the trading post had been fraught for Harvey. Shelton had been permanently on edge, barking commands and looking, always looking, for Hellfire's arrival.

Harvey had bitten his lip to avoid asking the questions he'd wanted to ask and which he knew Shelton didn't want to answer. Instead, he had carried out his duties quietly and spent whatever free time he had observing the sullen new arrivals.

These men had devoted themselves to silent contemplation of the approaching trail, filling the long hours in cleaning their guns with the studious attention of men who rely on their weapons to keep them alive.

Harvey had tried to find something to talk to them about, but his failed efforts only went to prove that a young assistant in a trading post had nothing in common with men who killed for a living.

'And what will you do when he comes?' Harvey asked.

Eli provided a wink which was so slight that Harvey thought it might have been a tic.

'What we have to do.'

Harvey nodded. 'And what's that?'

'Boy, you ask too many questions.'

Harvey rocked from foot to foot as he searched for something else to say. When he couldn't think of anything, he turned and left Eli, but as he passed Garth, Garth threw out an arm and grabbed Harvey's jacket, halting him, then lifted it high. He stared at his hip, then dropped the jacket.

'You not packing a gun yourself?' he asked.

'I can fire one, I surely can, but my uncle doesn't want me to learn that way of life.'

'A man's still got to protect himself.' Garth released the coat. 'Shelton's not your pa, then?'

'No. My parents died in Calamity's station fire.'

Garth nodded, a flash of sympathy appearing in his cold eyes. 'Sounds like you got a mighty powerful reason to want Hellfire dead for yourself.'

Harvey opened his mouth to try to sum up a lifetime of wondering what he'd do if he ever met

Hellfire, but from the post doorway, Shelton called for him.

'I've told you before,' Shelton said as Harvey joined him, 'I don't want you talking to those men.'

'I was just being friendly.'

'I'm sure you were, but these ain't friendly times and they ain't friendly people.' Shelton turned away to mutter under his breath, but then patted Harvey's shoulder and softened his voice. 'Just don't annoy them while they're working.'

Harvey nodded, then scuffed his feet from side to side as he searched for a way to ask the main question he'd wanted to ask ever since these men had arrived.

'And when they've finished working,' he whispered, 'are we moving on?'

'What you mean?'

Harvey sighed. 'You promised Eli a whole heap of money. But you haven't got that much money, and I thought that might mean you'll have to sell up.'

A smile twitched Shelton's mouth. 'Don't worry yourself. We're going nowhere.'

'But I *am* worried. You've always said this post will be mine one day. And I've often tried to work out how it makes money to pay for our keep, but I can't. And I can't see how you can afford to pay for hired guns.'

Shelton breathed deeply through his nostrils, his face reddening to take on a colour that was deeper than Harvey had ever seen.

'Enough, Harvey,' he snapped. 'It ain't your place to worry about things like that.'

'I'll try, uncle.' Harvey forced himself to provide a smile, then turned and looked along the ridge, his gaze centring on the rocky outcrop.

Shelton laid a friendly hand on his shoulder.

'And stop panicking,' he said, the anger gone from his voice. 'Perhaps I was wrong and Hellfire won't come, after all.'

'Perhaps.' Harvey shrugged. 'But it don't stop me looking.'

'You've done nothing but look for Hellfire for the last week. Don't think I don't notice.'

Harvey kicked at the dirt, wondering whether to raise his second most important question, but on glancing at the redness that still marred Shelton's face he just nodded and kept quiet.

Last week, he'd seen his mother's ghost again.

He'd first seen her as a child, but Shelton had told him it was just a rag caught on a tree, and sure enough, it didn't reappear the next night. But Harvey knew what he'd seen and whenever he was in distress, he would look out at sundown and she'd be standing on the outcrop, looking towards the trading post, her form silent and enigmatic, but strangely comforting.

Years had passed since he'd last been seriously worried, the nightmares of fires and infernos that had plagued his childhood having departed, but with the arrival of the hired guns, he'd been comforted to see her again.

And he was sure that mentioning this sighting

30

would result in the ghost leaving again and, in these troubled times, he couldn't face that. So, to avoid Shelton noticing where he was looking, he tore his gaze from the outcrop and looked down the trail.

He flinched and couldn't stop himself emitting a barked screech.

At least a dozen men were riding down the trail and heading straight for the post. Eli and his associates were already standing and watching them with interest.

'Someone's a-coming,' he murmured.

Shelton shivered, then looked over Harvey's shoulder. With a pronounced gulp, he stared at the approaching riders.

Harvey opened his mouth to ask if Hellfire were amongst them, but on seeing Shelton's wide-eyed stare, he closed his mouth instead.

CHAPTER 4

Stark Pass was silent as Lincoln led his men into town. He noted the saloon's broken window and the notice outside that it was closed until further notice. Several stores had closed shutters and the town presented none of the bustling atmosphere that Lincoln had heard it possessed.

At the town marshal's office he dismounted and, with his deputies trailing behind, headed across the boardwalk and backhanded the office door.

'Marshal Cooper,' he said, his voice echoing.

Inside, the marshal was pacing back and forth, cradling a bandaged hand, but he swung round to face the advancing Lincoln.

'Who wants him?' he asked, his voice shaking as he backed away.

Two paces in from the doorway Lincoln swung to a halt and slammed his hands on his hips.

'I do. I'm US Marshal Lincoln Hawk.'

Cooper blinked hard, then backed away another pace and pointed his bandaged hand at him.

'What. . . ? Where. . . ?'

'Ain't got time to waste on questions. An outlaw known as Hellfire has escaped. My guess is he's looking for the fifty thousand dollars that got away and to cause as much trouble as he can. I intend to give it to him before he gives it to anyone else.' Lincoln withdrew the notice of Hellfire's escape from his pocket and held it out to the marshal, but Cooper didn't even look at it.

'I . . . I . . . I don't want to get involved in anything like that.'

Lincoln advanced a long pace on Cooper.

'You don't? What kind of sorry-assed lawman are you?'

Cooper gulped, then shuffled sideways to his desk with his head down.

'The kind that runs this town. And you don't. Now, leave me alone.'

Lincoln glanced at Daniel, then at Alvin, receiving a bemused snort and a raised eyebrow, then turned back to Cooper.

'I ain't going nowhere. And I'm sure the citizens of Stark Pass will appreciate having some real lawmen in town. But Shelton Baez will be in danger first. He runs a trading post and I'll head on out there to check on him.' Lincoln looked Cooper up and down and sneered. 'You can come along if you promise not to get in my way.'

Cooper raised his head and met Lincoln's gaze as he pointed a shaking finger at him, the action shaking a globule of blood from his bandaged hand.

'This is my town and this is my—'

'Yeah, yeah, and it will be again when I've left,

but maybe after a few days with me, you'll learn how to act like a lawman.'

As Cooper lowered his head and muttered to himself, Daniel directed Lincoln to come to the window.

Lincoln kept his gaze on Cooper for a moment longer, then joined him. He peered outside to see that five men were striding down the road towards the office.

And every one of them had the look of a hired gun.

Shelton dragged Harvey into the trading post, but Eli hurried after him and slammed a hand on Shelton's shoulder, halting him.

'We came to stop Hellfire,' he said, 'not this many men.'

'He must have hired as many guns as he could find.' Shelton narrowed his eyes. 'But you can't mean to leave us.'

'Ain't staying around to face that many.' Eli turned and barked orders to his associates, Garth and Jackson, to move on out.

'I'll double the payment.' Shelton watched Eli pause, but then carry on. 'All right, I'll treble it.'

Eli glanced at Garth and Jackson, who both glanced at the approaching men, then provided nods.

As Shelton sighed with relief Garth took up a position in a hollow beside the corral. Jackson hurried inside and stood by the window. Eli encouraged Shelton to hide, but Shelton shook his

34

head and collected the gun he kept beneath the counter. He was a poor aim and a slow draw, but at short distances when his back was to the wall, he claimed he was as deadly as any man was.

Harvey nudged Shelton, his eyes bright.

'Uncle,' he said, 'you got a spare gun in the—'

'I never taught you the way of the gun,' Shelton said, not looking at him, 'and this ain't the time to start.'

Harvey murmured his disagreement, but Shelton busied himself with loading the gun and ignored his complaints. Then he ordered Harvey to kneel down behind the counter and, when Harvey complied, he joined Eli by the door.

But despite Shelton's orders Harvey edged back and forth behind the counter until he found a position that let him see through the window.

Outside, the riders pulled up twenty yards before the corral. As they spread out Shelton directed Eli to look at the rider with a red mark on the face.

'Get that one,' he said, 'and the rest will fall apart.'

As Eli nodded, that man, Hellfire, edged his horse forward a pace.

'Shelton Baez,' he shouted, 'come on out.'

'I ain't,' Shelton shouted. 'Now, just move on and leave me alone.'

Hellfire leaned forward in the saddle and chuckled.

'I've waited sixteen years for this. I ain't leaving without your hide.'

'Then you'll die here, like you should have done in Calamity.'

35

'Only person dying here is you, except it'll be a long and painful journey.' Hellfire spat to the side, but then sat back and directed his men to surround the post.

Inside, Shelton nodded to Eli and his hired guns blasted a sustained volley of gunfire at Hellfire's men. The first burst forced Hellfire to dismount in a hurry and scurry with his head down for the nearest cover, Shelton's buckboard.

Two of his men weren't so fast and Eli's deadly aim blasted them from their horses. But when the gunshot echoes faded, the bulk of Hellfire's men had gained cover.

Then they started a persistent bombardment of the post. When one volley ended the next began, letting neither Eli nor Jackson return anything more than sporadic retorts.

More than one shot ripped through the door and window and, with slugs tearing through the wooden walls, sparks of light spread across the pitted walls.

When one shot whistled across the post and broke a jug on the shelf above Harvey's head, Harvey threw himself to the floor and cowered behind the counter. But then in disgust at himself, he fast-crawled into the storeroom. He rummaged beneath a folded pile of cloth and a greased sheet of paper before emerging with the gun Shelton had told him not to use.

With the gun held close to his cheek he crawled across the floor and joined Shelton, who glared at the gun, then at him. Then gave a reluctant nod, although he did order him to stay away from the window.

Then three of Hellfire's men ran for the door. By the window, Jackson slammed a slug into one of the men's arms, which wheeled him to the ground. Outside, Garth leapt up to rip gunfire into the other man.

The second man went down, but the third man blasted lead into Garth's guts, forcing him to stagger back. Before he could right himself the wounded man tore lead into his chest from the ground.

Then he and a line of men ran to the post to press themselves to the wall and out of Harvey's view through the door.

Through gaps in the slats Harvey saw the outlines of the men, so he ventured out from the counter and fired, aiming to shoot them in the back through the wall. The shots were wild, but it did have the effect of forcing them away from the wall.

From the window Jackson fired, knocking one of these men to the ground, killing him instantly, then he ripped gunfire into the second man's guts. But, with a dying blast through the window, this man ripped a slug into Jackson's neck which wheeled him away from the window.

Eli's gaze swung to the side to see this and a stray bullet from outside tore into his shoulder forcing him to back into the post.

A cry of triumph came from outside. Although Harvey couldn't see what was happening he heard the firm patter of footfalls as Hellfire's men advanced on the post.

Shelton darted into the doorway and fired two quick and desperate shots, but when a hail of gunfire exploded, sending splinters from the wood cascading around him, he bleated and grabbed Harvey's arm. He dragged him back to the counter and, with the wounded Eli, they spread out, ready to make their last stand.

Outside, Hellfire shouted taunts, his men whooping their delight as they made their group sound as if it were twice the size while they fanned out before the post door.

Shelton glanced at Eli, who returned a wince and a slow shake of the head.

'Harvey,' Shelton said, his voice low and urgent, 'it's time for you to hide. Head to the dug-out and no matter what you hear, don't come out.'

'I won't run,' Harvey said. He knelt behind the counter and slammed both hands on the top, the gun held between them. He aimed at the door ready to take the first man who ventured through.

'You will,' Shelton said, considering Harvey's shaking hands. 'This is not your problem and you have to live to . . .'

Shelton reached under the counter and removed a wooden box, about six inches long and three inches high.

Harvey reckoned he'd seen everything in the post, but he'd never seen this small box before.

'What—'

Shelton raised a hand, silencing him, then pushed the box down the counter until it nudged Harvey's hand.

'Get this to . . . get this to her.'

Harvey took the box and fingered the plain sides, but then Shelton's instruction filtered through to his mind and he looked up.

'To *her*?'

Shelton looked down at Harvey. His eyes watered, but whether with an old memory or fear of what would happen, Harvey couldn't tell.

'You know, Harvey, you know.'

'But what do—'

'Just go, Harvey. You have to.'

Harvey and Shelton exchanged a long stare. Then Harvey threw himself into Shelton's arms and held on. He pulled back.

'Whatever happens, I want you to know that even though you weren't my real father, you brought me up real good and—'

'You got nothing you need to say to me. Now, head on out.' A burst of gunfire tore through the window, forcing them both to duck. On his knees, Shelton pointed to the storeroom. 'Now, go!'

Still Harvey wavered, but Shelton turned his back on him and hunkered down, the gun resting on the counter.

Harvey risked bobbing up to grab the box, then thrust it into his pocket and scurried into the storeroom. He didn't look back, knowing that even one glance would force him to stay.

On the run, he reached the back exit and threw open the door, but then skidded to a halt.

A shadow lay across the entrance.

Hellfire was blocking his way.

CHAPTER 5

Lincoln watched the hired guns head down the road. As they swung purposefully round to face the office he turned from the window to face Marshal Cooper.

'You know anything about these men?' he asked.

'No,' Cooper said, giving the approaching hired guns only the shortest of glances, 'and I don't take kindly to lawmen riding into my town and asking me questions.'

'Then, Marshal, I'll tell you what I think.' Lincoln beckoned for Cooper to join him at the window, then drew his gun. 'Hellfire is in search of a whole heap of money and news like that attracts hired guns. And I'll have to explain to them why they've made a big mistake.'

Cooper shuffled to the side to look around Lincoln.

'You're just plain trouble, Lincoln.'

'Sure am, and I reckon you'll learn plenty about being a lawman in the next two minutes.' Lincoln directed Daniel to take a position beside the door.

'Just keep your head down and you might live long enough to use it.'

Cooper darted his gaze at Lincoln, then at his deputies then at the men outside, who had now stopped in the middle of the road and were lining up before the office.

'All right,' he screeched, his eyes watering. 'They are with Hellfire and you can't let them know who you are. Just go while you still can and leave the talking to me.'

Lincoln snorted. 'I ain't going nowhere.'

'You have to.' Cooper looked to the ceiling, mouthing something to himself.

Lincoln glanced through the window. The sprawl of hired guns bunched to murmur to each other. A ripple of nodding passed between them, then they ran for cover to take up positions in the alley beside the law office and behind the barrels in front of the store on the opposite side of the road.

Lincoln took a deep breath then shouted after them.

'You men heard right. Marshal Lincoln Hawk is in town and if you reckon you're tough enough you'd better head on in here and get me. But it'll be the last thing you'll do.'

'You'll regret that taunt,' a man shouted from behind one of the barrels.

Lincoln glanced at Alvin and Daniel, conveying his orders silently, but as his deputies took up their positions Cooper slapped a hand on his shoulder then dragged him round. Lincoln sneered at him, then flinched on seeing Cooper's beseeching eyes. And when Cooper spoke, his voice was gruff and defeated.

'Don't take them on, Lincoln, don't.'

Lincoln shook his head. 'I don't let outlaws dictate to me.'

'But I do.'

'If that's *your* policy in *your* town, I ain't having nothing to do with it.'

'You will when Hellfire's kidnapped my family.' Cooper rubbed his eyes with the back of his bandaged hand. 'If I don't hand you over to those men outside, he'll kill my wife and children.'

Harvey threw the door closed with sufficient force to bundle Hellfire on to his back, then swirled round. He heard Hellfire cursing as he regained his feet. With no choice, Harvey scampered through the storeroom. Behind him, he heard the door crash open.

But then he skidded to a halt.

In the main room Shelton and Eli were making their last stand, but Hellfire's men were becoming bolder as they alternated between firing through the window and door. Their gunfire exploded across the post, ripping splinters from the counter and forcing Shelton and Eli to dive for cover.

Harvey glanced at his gun, wondering how he could prevail against such sustained fire, but the gun fell from his sweat-slickened hand and landed beside a double-doored cupboard. He moved to get it, but the creeping fear that was numbing his

42

mind had enforced clumsiness upon him and he banged his head on one of the cupboard doors.

Behind him, Hellfire was stomping closer. In desperation Harvey threw open the nearest cupboard door and leapt inside to hide in the corner.

The door swung closed. Through the gap between the cupboard doors he peered out as guns blazed across the post. A stray bullet ripped through the wood a foot above Harvey's head, forcing him to cringe himself into the smallest ball he could make.

But through the sliver of action he could see, he saw a bullet hammer into Eli's chest, splaying his body over the counter. Eli rolled from the counter, staggered a pace, then fell, slamming into the cupboard and splintering the wood. Then the cupboard rocked and came crashing down, landing on its front and half over his body.

Harvey flattened his hands over his ears, muffling the barked commands ripping out for Shelton to give himself up, but from the tone of Shelton's oath-filled replies, Harvey reckoned he'd fight to the last.

Then Hellfire's men stormed the post. Bullets flew everywhere, at least three thudding into Eli's body. Trapped in the cupboard, Harvey had no choice but to keep still and hope. Through the broken door he saw Eli's slack mouth and the pool of spreading blood.

'I got you trapped, Shelton,' Hellfire shouted.

'I ain't coming out, Hellfire,' Shelton shouted.

'I'll die before I surrender to you.'

A snort sounded. 'You ain't got the guts to fight to the death.'

Footfalls pounded across the post, then the sound of two men crashing together. A gunshot ripped out, then grunts and scuffing feet suggested a tussle.

Hellfire uttered a cry of triumph.

'Get your hands off me,' Shelton whimpered.

Hellfire snorted. 'I *was* right. You ain't got the courage to die.' A slap sounded, then the sound of a body hitting the floor. 'Now, where's the other one?'

'What other one?' someone asked.

'This runt tried to escape. He went back into the post. Find him!'

Harvey listened to Hellfire's men tip crates over and hurl boxes around the room. The clutter in the post was considerable, but Harvey held out no hope that they wouldn't find him.

Moving as quietly as he could, he squeezed his hand through the gap in the doors, feeling Eli's body and searching for his gun. But he felt only dampness and he was thankful that in the poor light, he couldn't see what he'd touched.

He listened to each crate falling, mentally picturing their progress around the post. And they were coming closer.

Then the cupboard shook as a man tried to lift it. Harvey held his breath, hoping that the man would consider the fallen cupboard as being some-where he wouldn't hide.

But the man called for another, Burl, to join him and, with a surge, they righted the cupboard. The doors clattered open then shut, but they were open long enough for the men outside to see Harvey.

Forlornly, Harvey cringed into the corner, but Hellfire threw open the doors and peered in at him. Then Burl's rough hands bundled him out and stood him straight.

'What you going to do with me?' Harvey murmured, daring to look up at Hellfire, but seeing no hope of mercy in his blemished face and blank eyes.

Hellfire snorted, then swirled round to face Shelton.

'This your son, Shelton?'

Shelton glanced at Harvey, his jaw set firm and his eyes displaying a coldness that Harvey knew was false.

'He ain't mine.'

Hellfire glanced from Shelton to Harvey, appraising them both, his blemish blazing.

'Then it won't concern you when I kill him.' Hellfire raised his gun and sighted Harvey's chest.

Harvey struggled, but on finding that Burl was holding him securely from the side, he puffed his chest and glared at Hellfire.

'He ain't no kin of mine,' Shelton murmured. 'But he doesn't deserve to die. He's done nothing to you.'

'He hasn't.' Hellfire fingered his chin, a smile emerging. 'But I can see in your eyes that you have

45

a connection to him.'

'It's called humanity. Something you know nothing about.'

'You're wrong there. But you got ten seconds to tell me about the fifty thousand dollars that went missing.' Hellfire licked his lips. 'Or I'll kill him.'

Shelton gulped. 'I know nothing about that. I was in the station getting nearly burned to death with the rest of your other victims.'

'But you didn't. You got out alive. And I reckon you know what happened to that money.'

'That's a big guess and you know it.'

'It is a guess.' Hellfire roved his gun in a circle, aiming at Harvey's head, then chest, then head again. 'But if I'm wrong, it'll cost you this young man's life.'

Shelton gulped, his breath coming short and hard.

'If you want to know what happened back at that station, ask Marshal Billy Epstein. He's retired now, but that man was as useless as any lawman I've ever met and if someone spirited that money away, it was him.'

'Marshal Epstein,' Hellfire mused. He glanced at several of his men, received a variety of snorts and muttered comments, then clicked his fingers.

A grunted series of orders passed between Hellfire's men before being relayed outside. With Hellfire looking to the door, Harvey followed the direction of his gaze and winced on seeing Billy Epstein pace into the post. But Billy was glaring at Shelton, and when he reached him he backhanded his cheek, rocking his head to the side.

Hellfire chuckled, then swirled round to face Harvey.

'If Shelton won't plead for your life, will you?' he demanded.

'Never,' Harvey grunted, then firmed his jaw and coughed to eliminate the tremor in his voice. 'I've forgiven you for what you did to me a long time ago.'

Hellfire's right eye twitched. 'Forgiven me?'

'You burnt down Calamity's station and killed my—'

'I didn't burn down that station and I lost more than . . .' Hellfire looked to the ceiling, his breathing coming in harsh snorts. Then he lowered his head to look at Harvey, a maniacal gleam in his eye. 'But I'm afraid you won't be so lucky today.' Hellfire flashed a smile. 'You get to live.'

He barked an order to Burl and, with Billy's help, they bundled him into a chair.

Harvey struggled, but they clamped firm hands on his shoulders then secured him to the chair with thick bonds. When they stood back, Harvey flashed a glance over his shoulder at Shelton, but Hellfire pushed his head to the side and forced him to face the back of the post.

With his jaw set firm, Harvey listened. Then a chuckle sounded.

'No!' Shelton cried, but a sharp slap echoed across the post. Then Hellfire dragged him outside, Shelton screeching and pleading at every pace.

Behind him, Harvey heard Hellfire's men scamper out after him, but Burl stayed back in the post. Harvey strained his hearing, wondering what he was doing, but as far as he could tell he just pattered around the post.

The back of Harvey's neck burned as he anticipated whatever Burl was going to do to him, but deep in the pit of his stomach a faint hope burgeoned that he would leave him alive.

Then the door slammed shut. Scraping and thudding sounded, as of someone placing a barrier across the door.

With a long breath held deep in his chest, Harvey tensed, listening and confirming that he was now alone.

But Hellfire's men were still moving around outside.

Harvey closed his eyes and took a deep breath, trying to gulp down the fear that had clamped his throat.

Then he heard a crackle, and another.

Harvey forced his head to turn as far as it would go, straining to see the small amount of the post that was visible to him. And the part of the floor that he could see was well-lit, far more than the interior darkness should allow.

But that light flickered and, with a flash of shocked heat, he realized what was happening.

Hellfire was torching the post.

'So,' Lincoln said, 'if these men reckon you're helping me, Hellfire will kill your family?'

Cooper wrung his bandaged hand. 'That's the way it is.'

'Then I guess you'd better stay out his.'

Lincoln glanced away, but then swirled round, his fist snapping up to connect with Cooper's jaw and send him reeling into his desk. The marshal folded over the desk to lie sprawled on the other side. Lincoln watched him long enough to ensure he was out cold, then turned to look through the office window.

He saw one of the hired guns leap up from behind a barrel and blast at the office, the lead winging through the window and sending glass flying.

Lincoln ducked and waited for the barrage to end, then bobbed up. He saw that the hired gun was still standing, so he blasted a slug through the broken window. With deadly accuracy it ripped into the man's chest and slammed him back against the wall. A second slug to the head whirled him round to lie sprawled over the barrel with his arms dangling.

Then the road descended into quiet. Lincoln pressed himself flat to the wall to peer down the road but saw none of the other hired guns. He glanced at Alvin, who shrugged.

'Perhaps they're trying to outflank us,' Alvin said.

'Or perhaps they got sense and ran,' Daniel said from the other side of the window.

Lincoln shrugged. 'Or they might have gone to fetch reinforcements.'

As Alvin and Daniel winced Lincoln gestured to them, delivering orders that didn't require words. He counted to three on raised fingers. Then the lawmen hurried from the office with their guns brandished.

Alvin went left, Daniel went right, and Lincoln headed straight out into the road. Daniel and Alvin hunkered down, covering most of the left- and right-hand sides of the road.

Lincoln swirled round on the spot, looking for the other men. Then, down the alley, he saw a gun protruding into the road. He blasted a single shot at the gun, ripping shards from the wall and forcing the man to back into the alley.

Then he saw movement on the law office roof. Two men had scaled the roof and were edging to the front.

'On high,' Lincoln shouted.

On their knees, Alvin and Daniel swung round and fired up at the roof. Alvin hit the first man in the chest, the man tumbled forwards over the false-front to slam into the dirt beside him, but the second man got in a wild shot that ripped past Lincoln's leg.

Lincoln steadied his aim, then fired, knocking the man back. As the man stood straight with the blow, both Daniel and Alvin ripped gunfire into him which crashed him on to his back. He slid from the roof and thudded to the boardwalk below.

Lincoln counted through their successes and decided two more men remained, but even as he peered up at the roof looking for them, Alvin and Daniel blasted a volley of shots behind him.

He swirled round to see a man fly backwards through the store window, his hands clutching his reddening chest.

And that just left the man in the alley.

Lincoln gestured with his hands facing down, signifying that they would try to take this man alive, then hurried to the side of the alley. There he waited, and sure enough, the gun slipped out from the alley.

The man fired, but Lincoln aimed at the gun, winging it from his grasp. The force dragged the man's arm out from the alley and Lincoln lunged for that arm, then yanked him out on to the board-walk.

He gained a firmer grip, then stood him straight and slugged his jaw.

The man crashed on to his back, but Lincoln was on him in an instant. He grabbed his collar, pulled him high, and slammed his gun barrel right between his eyes.

'Mortimer T. Foster,' he said, 'I never thought I'd see your ugly hide again.'

'Lincoln Hawk,' Mortimer snarled, his gaze never leaving Lincoln's face, 'Hellfire will make you pay for this.'

'I don't think so. Now, do you want me to blast you away, or will you take me to Hellfire?'

'I guess you'll just have to kill me. I ain't double-crossing Hellfire.'

'Then maybe I'll just . . .' Lincoln firmed his

gun hand, his finger tightening the trigger as he stared into Mortimer's eyes. But then, with a huge grin, Lincoln lowered his gun. 'I'll just let you go.'

'Lincoln,' Alvin said.

'Don't worry.' Lincoln dragged Mortimer to his feet and stood him straight. 'Mortimer is going to deliver a message to Hellfire.'

'And the message?' Mortimer said, hope alighting in his eyes despite his arrogance.

'Tell Hellfire this is between him and me. It always was and it always will be. Tell him there's only one place we could ever meet to end this, and I'll expect him there at sundown.'

'And where's that?'

Lincoln swung Mortimer round and kicked his rump, knocking him into the road.

'Hellfire knows.'

CHAPTER 6

Harvey struggled but the thick bonds around his wrists meant he couldn't move his hands.

He glanced at the fire, which was licking at the crates and rising ever higher towards the ceiling. It would be only minutes before the post was an inferno. With a growing emptiness in his stomach he struggled against his bonds, but they were tight.

For a second he closed his eyes to force calm, then he glanced down. Hellfire's men had tied his legs together and his hands behind his back. But, although they had tied his hands to the chair, they hadn't tied his feet to the chair legs.

Harvey rocked back and forth, then mustered a huge push that rolled him to his feet. He steadied himself, then hopped forward. Ignoring the bloodied and heaped bodies of the gunslingers whom Shelton and Eli had dispatched, he shuffled across the post to the door, then leaned against it.

But the door didn't move.

He hammered against the door with his shoulders, but couldn't move the solid wood and whatever obstruction Hellfire had placed over the door. With a terrible burst of fear dampening his brow and making his heart race, he slumped back into the chair and thrust his legs up at the door. He strained, pushing his legs forwards. The door creaked, but it didn't move.

He rejected this escape method and rocked to his feet, then shuffled round to face away from the door and leapt backward. The chair cut into his legs and his hands dug deep into the small of his back, but he ignored the pain and repeated the action.

This time, a crack sounded and the chair partially collapsed beneath him. Not holding back this time, he leapt at the door and the chair collapsed into firewood beneath him.

Although unencumbered by the chair, his arms and thighs were still bound. He glanced over his shoulder. Flames licked at the ceiling, which blackened and shrank from the blaze.

With painful coughs racking his chest, Harvey abandoned his attempt to batter down the door. Fire had already blocked his route to the back exit so he shuffled to the window instead. Without time to work out how to rip the rope from his thighs, he leapt against the wooden shutters, but they held as fast as the door had.

Harvey glanced at the ceiling, which was reddening. Motes of black soot cascaded down. He blinked to clear his watering eyes, but cloying smoke was fogging his vision. Then through his watering eyes he saw the circles of light that the sustained gunfire had ripped into the wooden walls.

And in one plank several holes were close together.

In utter desperation Harvey hurled his shoulder at this spot. He heard a crack deep within the wood and he hurled himself again. It might have been his imagination, but this time he was sure he felt the wall give a little.

He slammed his shoulder against the wall again and heard another crack, but it was no louder than before, so Harvey searched around on the floor. The only object he found that might help him break out was a poker. He knelt and rolled on to his back. The poker stuck into the small of his back. Desperate seconds passed as he tried to wiggle it into his hands.

Lying on his back, he saw the roof was alight. Waves of flame rippled along the underside. Flurries of soot rained down in burning flakes. The heat grew by the moment, drying his sweat instantly and baking his face.

He gave a cry of relief as the poker slipped into his hands. He rolled to his feet. As the smoke burned his throat he gulped, but the effort didn't help his parched throat. He shook his head to rid himself of a growing desire to sleep and bounded to the wall, turned, then manoeuvred the poker between two planks. With a wrenching tug, he spun away.

Wood splintered and pulled away. Wasting no time, Harvey raised the poker higher and repeated the action. Another strip of wood splintered, letting him see outside, but the remainder of the plank was solid and it was higher than he could raise his bound hands.

Harvey dropped the poker then rolled to the ground and wriggled, forcing his hands to the backs of his heels. He dragged them beneath his boots to his front.

With more freedom of movement he grabbed the poker and yanked along the plank, levering away whole sections of wood. When he'd cleared a one-yard length he started on the plank below. With the additional leverage afforded by the gap he was able to splinter the wood away.

He coughed as an intense wave of heat rippled across his back. He was sure he could feel blisters breaking out, but he gritted his teeth and concentrated on the plank.

Then, behind him, a huge crash sounded as the roof collapsed.

Half-blinded by the thickening smoke, he put all his strength into one muscle-ripping pull. In an explosion of splinters, he dragged away the next plank. Behind him the heat was intense, burning his back and singeing his clothes. With no choice, he thrust his head through the gap. It was too small to slip through but, with one last desperate shove, he forced his shoulders through, ripping out more wood as he half-threw, half-fell through the gap to freedom.

While Harvey floundered on the ground outside, dragging in cooling gasps of air, a huge plume of smoke exploded through the hole as the ceiling collapsed.

Then he remembered that Hellfire could still be outside.

Coughing so badly he thought he'd be sick, he groped on the ground and grabbed the poker. He stood defiant, waiting for Hellfire to try to force him inside.

He waited, but only the occasional bird-call greeted him. He glared in a steady arc across the plains. They were as peaceful as they had been before Hellfire arrived.

But to his side he saw movement.

Harvey swirled round and, as he'd half-expected, saw the caped figure standing on the rocky outcrop, its form looking down at the burning post.

Despite everything, Harvey smiled to himself, then turned and walked towards the figure.

The outlaw Mortimer Foster edged away from Lincoln, his uncertain steps suggesting he couldn't believe that Lincoln would really let him go. But Lincoln gave an encouraging nod and he danced back, then scurried for his horse.

He mounted his steed, then turned it and headed down the road, but as he gained open land on the edge of town, a bullet ripped out from behind Lincoln and tore into Mortimer's side, knocking him sideways.

Lincoln swirled round to see that Marshal Cooper had regained consciousness and now stood in the office doorway, his gun drawn and smoking. Lincoln thrust up his arm to grab the marshal's and send his second shot high in the air, then he swirled round. He saw Mortimer slip from his saddle. Then one foot became caught in a stirrup. He was dragged after his horse. And, as he bounced out of town without attempting to regain the saddle, Lincoln reckoned he was dead.

'What you do that for?' Lincoln demanded.

'He was getting away,' Cooper said.

'And I wanted him to. I'd thrown down my challenge to Hellfire.'

'It's not your place to do that. This ain't your investigation.'

'It ain't. But how did killing that man help?'

Cooper felt his jaw as he paced out on to the boardwalk.

'Knocking me out to keep me away from the fight wouldn't convince that man I wasn't helping you. So, he would have reported what he saw to Hellfire and he'd have killed my family, just as he'd threatened to.'

Lincoln snorted a deep breath through his nostrils, but then nodded grudgingly.

He let Cooper return to his office, then gestured for his deputies to follow him in. But he waited to watch the townsfolk emerge from hiding for the first time since he'd returned to Stark Pass. He gestured to them in a placating way to let them know this crisis was over. Several people gestured back at him and Lincoln was pleased to recognize many of them from his previous time in the area.

58

But amongst the faces there was one man he wasn't pleased to see. Marshal Billy Epstein was alone outside the saloon, mounted on a horse which, from its sweating flanks, Lincoln reckoned he'd just ridden into town. And even if his wizened form suggested he'd ceased to be a lawman for some years, Lincoln still had nothing but contempt for him after his role in the events of sixteen years ago.

And from Billy's sneer and the way he snapped the reins around, then rode out of town, he guessed the feeling was mutual.

Lincoln watched him until he'd swung round the last buildings on the edge of town, noting that he was heading north, then turned to the law office.

'North,' he murmured to himself, the hint of a long-dormant memory tapping at his thoughts. 'There ain't nothing north of Stark Pass worth visiting except the caves in Wildman's Gulch.'

CHAPTER 7

'You ready to talk?' Hellfire asked as he paced towards the cringing Shelton.

With a hand raised to fend off any blows, Shelton back-kicked along the ground until he banged his head against the cave wall. He peered up at Hellfire, then ran his gaze across his twenty or so men. He saw no hint of mercy in any of their eager grins.

In their midst were three other hostages: Leah Cooper and her two small children. Shelton looked at them, hoping to share a moment of compassion with another decent person, but they didn't look at him.

At his side was a cage, about six-foot high and four-foot square, the bars solid iron. Shelton tried not to look at the heavy lock on the door and the manacles dangling from the top.

'I ain't got nothing to say to you,' he murmured, returning his gaze to Hellfire.

'Now that ain't friendly,' Hellfire said, pouting his bottom lip with mock indignation.

'Quit mocking me and tell me what you want.'

'I want you to talk. Then I want you to die.' Hellfire glanced at the cage and grinned. 'And I'll get that wish soon.'

Shelton gulped to moisten his rapidly drying throat.

'What you going to do?' he murmured, then bit his bottom lip in irritation at voicing his fear.

'I haven't decided.' With his movements steady, Hellfire reached down and drew a knife from his boot. He glanced at the blade. 'It depends on how quickly you talk. Fifty thousand dollars went missing. It should have been on the train, but it wasn't. And I have it on good authority that you know where that money went.'

'Billy Epstein,' Shelton snorted, 'wasn't a reliable source of information sixteen years ago and he ain't now.'

'I know that.' Hellfire slammed his boot to the cave wall beside Shelton's face and leaned on his knee to peer down at him. 'But I trust my methods of making people talk, and I reckon I can make you suffer the equivalent of sixteen years of prison in one day.'

'You didn't go to prison because of me. You went for all the ... all the trouble you caused in Calamity.'

'But without you speaking up that wouldn't have happened.' Hellfire glanced at his knife, then stabbed at the cave wall. A flurry of grit escaped to cascade on to Shelton's head. 'I've heard it said that you can keep a man alive for days, making a

61

nick here and a nick there.'

Hellfire continued to stab at the wall, his actions becoming stronger and stronger, but then he hurled the knife away for it to stab into the dirt.

'Or then again,' he continued, glancing at the fire in the cave entrance, 'I might do something even worse.'

'Hellfire, you got to believe me. I was with you when you torched . . .' Shelton gulped. '. . . when that fire broke out. I know nothing about the fifty thousand dollars. I know nothing about nothing.'

Hellfire lowered his leg to the ground and stepped back to appraise Shelton.

'You calling the death of my woman nothing?'

'Your woman?' Shelton intoned.

'Yeah, my woman – Adele.'

Shelton furrowed his brow. 'You mean that whore you kidnapped and—'

'That was no whore!' Hellfire roared, spit flying from his mouth to splatter Shelton's face. 'She was a fine woman and she was my woman.'

A nervous giggle broke out from one of Hellfire's men and Hellfire swirled round to confront him.

'What you laughing at?' he roared, his voice echoing in the cave.

The man glanced around, searching everyone's eyes, perhaps for support, but receiving nothing but sad shakes of heads and an almost imperceptible shuffling away from him to leave him standing alone.

'Nothing,' he murmured, looking at his feet.

'Then what were you laughing at?'

'I . . . I . . . I guess Shelton was right, I guess.' He took a deep breath. 'From what I've heard Adele wasn't exactly—'

Hellfire roared with anger, then stormed across the cave.

The man backed, throwing his hands before his face, but Hellfire still lunged and grabbed his throat. He marched him to the cave wall and, with his back braced, raised him from the ground. The man struggled but Hellfire had grabbed a firm grip of his throat and held him against the wall.

The man battered Hellfire's fists, but his face darkened and the blows landed with reducing force. He darted his gaze around, his eyes boggling, but nobody moved to help him and Hellfire just dragged him higher up the cave wall until his arm was fully outstretched.

'Tell me about Adele. Tell me she was a fine woman. Tell me! Tell me!'

The man battered at Hellfire's arms but his grip was so tight that the blood had drained from the knuckles. The man opened and closed his mouth but only a pained screech emerged, along with his lolling tongue.

'I said,' Hellfire roared, 'tell me!'

Hellfire thrust up his arm to its utmost and, with a last bubbling moan, the man went limp. Hellfire still held on for a full minute, his head cocked to one side and still demanding an answer. Then he snorted and hurled the limp body away. It landed in a crumpled heap. Hellfire batted his hands together, then stepped over it and confronted his huddle of men.

'Anyone else got anything to say about my woman?'

As Hellfire's men studiously avoided catching his eye, Shelton shuffled into the base of the cave wall, trying to make his form as small as possible in the forlorn hope that maybe this distraction would keep Hellfire from noticing him. And, almost as if he *had* forgotten, Hellfire strode away from him and through the parting group of men to stand over his other hostages.

By the light of the fire at the front of the cave Shelton could see that Hellfire was now smiling, all signs of his former raging anger fading as he hunkered down before Leah.

'How are you?' he said.

Leah darted her gaze around the cave before she looked at him, then clutched the two children closer to her chest.

'We'll be fine as soon as you release us,' she said, a tremor in her voice despite her defiance.

'And I ain't doing that until your husband's finished helping me.' Hellfire reached out to finger a lock of the elder child's hair. 'Which he will if he wants to see these charming children again.'

'Stay away from her,' Leah muttered.

'Relax. I wouldn't hurt a child.' Hellfire leaned down and brushed the curl to the side. 'What's your name, little one?'

'I'm Mollie,' the girl whispered, her voice small and scared.

'You're not scared of me, are you?'

Mollie glanced up at her mother, then gave a shrug.

'No,' she mumbled. 'I guess.'

'You guess? You don't sound sure. How can I persuade you I'm a nice man?'

'Letting us go would help,' Leah murmured.

Hellfire flashed her a harsh glare, then softened his expression as he looked at Mollie.

'Perhaps we could play a game. That might make you laugh.' He winked at Mollie, then clapped his mouth while making silly faces until she giggled and nodded. He clicked his fingers above his head. 'Three mugs.'

The man who Shelton reckoned was Hellfire's closest confidant, Burl, dashed to the back of the cave and returned with three mugs. Hellfire set them on the ground before Mollie, then reached into his shirt and unhooked a locket from his neck, which he placed beneath the middle mug.

'What's the game?' Mollie asked, her eyes brightening for the first time.

'You have to guess where the locket is. And if you do, you'll get to keep it.'

Hellfire lifted the middle mug to show her that the locket was still there, then shuffled the mug to the side and around the right-hand mug. Then he took the left-hand mug in his left hand and moved the mugs in a figure-of-eight pattern.

All the time Mollie kept her gaze on the mug with the locket under it. And when Hellfire sat back and raised his hands, she giggled, then tapped the central mug. But when Hellfire tipped the mug over, there was nothing beneath it.

Mollie knuckled her eyes. 'I watched. It has to be there.'

'Then you shouldn't have taken the locket.' Hellfire winked then reached out to cup her ear. He pulled back to reveal the locket in his hand. 'You had it behind your ear all along.'

'I don't . . . I was sure it . . .' She grinned. 'Show me again.'

Hellfire chuckled. 'This time, watch the mugs more closely.'

He shuffled the mugs in a convoluted pattern. In the cave entrance Hellfire's men started muttering to each other. Outside, a horse neighed, but Hellfire remained hunched over the mugs, his concentration centred on Mollie's rapt expression as he circled the mugs around each other.

Then fast footfalls pattered. Shelton looked to the side to see Billy Epstein scurry through the entrance. Burl hailed Hellfire, but Hellfire swirled round, his eyes blazing.

'Don't interrupt me,' he grunted, 'when I'm entertaining my favourite little girl.'

'But it's that marshal,' Burl said. 'And he don't look happy.'

Hellfire leaned over the mugs, snorting, then slapped them to the side. His hand whirled as he pocketed the locket, then he flashed Mollie an apologetic smile and stood to face the cave entrance.

Billy walked through the milling outlaws to face Hellfire.

'What's wrong?' Hellfire asked, his blazing eyes suggesting that the price of a poor answer would be terminal.

'Marshal Lincoln Hawk,' Billy said, 'that's what wrong. He arrived and took out all the men you left in town. But he tried to give you a message. He wants to meet you and end this.'

'Where?'

'I'd only just arrived back in town when the shooting started. I managed to snoop around in an alley but didn't hear everything he said. But I reckon he said that you'd know.'

Hellfire licked his lips, then gave a slow nod.

'I guess I do.' He shrugged. 'And Marshal Cooper?'

'He killed Mortimer,' Billy said. 'He's double-crossed you.'

Hellfire flared his eyes as he looked at Leah, but Leah shook her head.

'He wouldn't endanger . . .' she said, her voice trailing off to shocked silence.

'But he has.' Hellfire paced round on the spot to stare down at Leah, who drew her children closer to her chest.

'Don't do anything,' she pleaded, cringing.

'I won't harm *you*.' Hellfire hunkered down beside the children. He looked at Mollie, a huge smile on his lips. 'You enjoyed playing with me, didn't you?'

'Yes, sir,' Mollie said.

'Yes, sir,' Hellfire said, nodding. 'As you're so polite, we could play another game. You say the rhyme: *round and round I go and where my finger stops nobody knows.*' Hellfire pointed at himself, then at Mollie with each word. 'And when your finger stops, whoever you're pointing at is the winner.'

Mollie giggled. Then she started the rhyme.

'Round and round,' she said, her small voice loud in the silence that had descended on the cave as she pointed at herself then at Hellfire.

'But I've already played the game,' Hellfire said. 'This time, play it with your baby sister.'

Mollie nodded, then restarted the rhyme.

'Round and round I go,' she said, her small finger pointing to herself then at her sister. 'And where my finger stops nobody knows.'

She chortled and clapped her hands when she stopped the rhyme with her finger pointing at herself.

'You won,' Hellfire said.

Mollie clapped her hands. 'What have I won?'

Hellfire just grinned.

Lincoln knocked back the dregs of his coffee, then sat back in his chair.

It had been three hours since the gunfight and he had the growing feeling that his assumption that the skirmish would have attracted a man who could never avoid a confrontation was wrong.

Cooper wandered to him, his eyes downcast, and refilled his coffee.

'Obliged.' Lincoln considered the lawman. 'And I understand your problem. But that won't

68

stop me telling you that you shouldn't have helped Hellfire.'

Cooper slumped down on the edge of his desk and considered Lincoln, his eyes watery and dull.

'I had to. Hellfire gave me no choice.'

'You always have a choice.' Lincoln leaned forward. 'But if we work together we can find Hellfire and free your family.'

Cooper glanced at his bandaged hand. When he spoke his voice was low.

'All right.'

Lincoln softened his expression and lowered his voice.

'Now, tell me everything you know about their capture.'

Cooper nodded, but as he opened his mouth Alvin, from by the window, grunted.

Lincoln and Cooper headed across the room to see a rider hurtle by outside. The rider reached behind him, then hurled a package which thudded into the door.

Everyone scurried away from the door, but when thirty seconds had passed and the explosion they'd all feared hadn't materialized, Lincoln peered through the window. The package still lay on the boardwalk.

He opened the door and looked up and down the road, his gun drawn and thrust out before him, but the man who had hurled the package was already galloping out of town, heading north.

Lincoln hefted the package, feeling a heavy and possibly moist object slither around inside as he slipped back into the law office. He placed the package on Cooper's desk and moved to open it, but Cooper shooed him away.

'I've had enough of your interfering,' he murmured.

Lincoln backed across the room. His deputies were looking at him with their eyebrows raised, but Lincoln just shrugged.

Cooper slit open the package with a knife and, with the corner lifted, peered inside. He gulped and slammed the lid closed then slumped into his chair. His undamaged hand came up to hold his chin, but it was shaking so much he slumped to lie with his face buried in his arms.

A sob escaped his lips.

Lincoln joined him and, with slow movements, reached out to take the package. Cooper didn't look at him, his body convulsing with sobs. So Lincoln raised a corner of the lid, then grimaced and let it fall back down.

Alvin and Daniel were heading towards him, but Lincoln raised a hand, halting them.

'It's a baby,' he murmured, 'a dead—'

'That ain't just a baby,' Cooper roared, snapping up to confront Lincoln. 'That's my child, and Hellfire's gone and hacked it to pieces because I helped you. My child is lying there all mutilated and torn because of you.'

'I did nothing that'd—'

'Quit answering back.' Cooper leaned forward, rising on his heels to meet Lincoln's gaze, but then he swirled round and hammered his undamaged hand on his desk.

'Alvin,' Lincoln said, his voice low, 'get him a whiskey.'

Alvin located a bottle of whiskey in a cupboard. He poured a drink then held it out to the marshal.

Cooper shrugged away from the glass, but when Lincoln insisted he gulped down half the drink, then hurled the glass away for it to smash against the wall.

'I ain't drinking my way out of this.'

'I never said you should.'

'But you did this, Lincoln.' Cooper pointed at the box. 'You did this.'

'If you think that's true, I'm sorry.'

'Sorry ain't good enough. Your gun-toting ways killed her. You rode into my town and you only thought of yourself and your gun and your target. You didn't care about who else suffered.'

'I did, believe me. And if there was anything I could have done to stop this, I would have, but—'

'I don't want to hear the buts.' Cooper pointed at the door, his finger firm. 'You'll leave my town now and you won't ever come back.'

Lincoln backed away a short pace, then stopped and held his hands wide.

'You need my help to save the rest of your family.'

'I don't,' Cooper roared and stormed across the office to stand before Lincoln, his face bright red and his fists raised. 'Get out before I kill you with my bare hands!'

CHAPTER 8

'I can't believe we're really going,' Alvin said as he mounted his horse.

But Lincoln set his gaze forward as he led his deputies out of Stark Pass at a steady trot.

'Cooper gave me no choice,' he said when they reached the edge of town.

'Yeah, but despite everything, we have the right to—'

'Sometimes right don't matter,' Lincoln snapped, swirling round in the saddle. 'Cooper's grieving awful bad and we got to leave him.'

Lincoln saw Alvin and Daniel glance at each other, but he turned to face the front.

'Then it seems like we really are going,' Alvin murmured.

They rode out of town, but rather than heading towards the rail track and the route back east Lincoln headed west. His deputies murmured to each other, but Lincoln didn't feel inclined to explain his reasoning.

He remained silent until they were ten miles out

of Stark Pass. When he was near to cresting a familiar incline before a long ridge he issued orders to his deputies to be on their guard.

Before they reached the top of the knoll he saw the plume of smoke rising ahead.

Lincoln speeded his horse down the other side. Within two minutes he saw the blackened skeleton of the building. He realized that the smoke was the dying remnants of a fire and not a recent happening. He drew his horse to a halt and stared at the wrecked trading post, his jaw set firm. Then turned to Alvin.

'That's Shelton Baez's trading post.' He sighed. 'Or at least it used to be.'

'Seems Hellfire got there ahead of us.' Alvin winced, then raised the reins. 'We'd better check it out.'

'No need,' Lincoln said. 'We don't need to confirm what we'll find there.'

Alvin still edged his horse forwards, then nodded and turned his back on the post.

'Was Shelton Baez the only surviving witness to what happened in Calamity sixteen years ago?'

'Yeah, aside from me and . . .' Lincoln turned to Alvin, then looked over his shoulder at Daniel. 'You both heard what Marshal Cooper said. We got no right interfering in his investigation, and even if we had, he's got kin at stake and he doesn't want my help.'

'We know that,' Alvin said.

'I know your views that we should do something anyhow, but you got to know this ain't about

73

Hellfire and it ain't about Cooper's kin. This is about Hellfire and me. And I can't ask you to join me.'

Alvin smiled. 'So you are going after Hellfire, after all?'

Lincoln gave a short nod.

Daniel and Alvin looked at each other, then turned to Lincoln.

'Then so are we,' Daniel said.

Lincoln nodded and, without further word, swung his horse around. He galloped north, his deputies hurrying to keep up with him.

They galloped in an arc around Stark Pass, crossing the railroad tracks five miles out of town. When they reached the main trail north, Lincoln continued along it until he reached a point where the trail wended a path through a phalanx of boulders.

He directed Alvin to take a look-out position on the top of the smallest of the boulders. Then he and Daniel waited beside a heap of boulders that protected them from the view of anyone riding south.

They waited quietly. Both deputies had worked with Lincoln before and they didn't need to ask him what his plan was, trusting that whatever hunch he was backing would explain itself in due course.

And sure enough, after an hour of patient waiting Alvin waved down at Lincoln and raised a finger. Lincoln returned a nod.

'Billy Epstein,' he mouthed to Daniel.

The lawmen edged to the side of the trail. Presently Billy trotted through the boulders. But on seeing Lincoln standing by the trail he flinched. He moved to turn his horse round and head back north, but Alvin had already jumped down on to the trail behind him and blocked his way.

While Billy was still undecided as to what to do Lincoln dashed down the trail and blocked his forward route. Daniel grabbed the horse's reins.

Billy struggled, trying to tear the reins away, but when Lincoln drew his gun and sighted on his chest, he relented and let Daniel lead his horse towards Lincoln, who smiled up at him.

'Billy Epstein,' he said, 'I've been waiting for you.'

'I was on business,' Billy murmured. 'And you got no right stopping me from going about that business.'

'You're right. I got no right to do nothing.' Lincoln glanced at his gun, then swirled it into his holster, but he raised his hand and clenched it into a tight fist. 'Unless you've broken the law, then I got every right to drag you off that horse and deal with you.'

'I used to be a town marshal. I ain't ever broken no law.'

Lincoln raised his eyebrows. 'And there's me reckoning that you were returning from Wildman's Gulch, a well known spot for outlaws to hole up in. And a spot where Hellfire might have made a base.'

'I resent the—' Billy screeched as Alvin slammed a hand on his waist and pulled him down from his horse, then stood him straight and facing Lincoln.

'I could have meant I thought you were searching for him. Why did you think I meant you met him?'

Billy gulped. 'You can't prove nothing.'

'But a box back in Stark Pass proves somebody saw Hellfire. You'd better hope nobody suggests to Marshal Cooper that it was you.'

'Then I got no problem,' Billy murmured, not meeting Lincoln's eye. 'It wasn't me.'

'But you do know where Hellfire is hiding out.' Lincoln advanced a long pace on Billy with his fist raised. 'And you will tell me.'

'I'll tell you nothing,' Billy grunted, firming his jaw.

'My methods aren't as brutal as Hellfire's are, but I reckon I can make you talk.' Lincoln slapped his fist into his palm with a resounding crack. 'I'd save yourself some pain and just talk.'

'I got a box for you,' Harvey shouted as he scampered up the slope and away from the post.

But the caped figure was still over 200 yards ahead of him.

He had taken fifteen minutes to wriggle out of the ropes that had encased his legs and, as yet, hadn't found a way to remove the ropes from his hands. And in that time the figure had slipped back from the outcrop.

But it was now moving away along the top of the

ridge, skirting away from the post, its slow speed just keeping it ahead of him and taunting Harvey.

He waved the box above his head and shouted again, but the caped figure didn't look back.

Harvey tried to put on a burst of speed, but a sharp pain ripped through his chest and he staggered to a halt. With his head lolling, he coughed, freeing his lungs of the cloying tang of smoke.

When he'd regained his breath he looked up; the figure was cresting the summit of the ridge and disappearing from view. Without much hope, he shuffled after it, his pace gradually building into a shambling run.

But it was another ten minutes before he crested the ridge and when he peered over the other side the terrain ahead of him was barren. He couldn't see the figure.

He stood with his hands to his brow, searching the landscape, but saw only rocks, the afternoon heat haze making their forms shimmer. Despite the sun's beating down on his head and his narrow escape from the fire, he shivered.

'Who are you?' he shouted. 'Where are you going? What do you want?'

But his voice was lost in the vastness.

He kept his gaze on the barren wilderness, searching for movement, but not even a bird moved before him. So, with a shake of the head, he headed back down the side of the ridge, aiming to return to the post.

But then marks in the dirt caught his eye.

He shuffled closer and saw that the marks were

footprints. He hunkered down beside them, even fingering them to prove they were real, then rolled back on to his haunches and nodded to himself.

'I don't know who you are, where you've gone, or what you want,' he said to himself. 'But I do know you ain't no ghost.'

CHAPTER 9

'There's not as many as I expected,' Alvin said, peering over the top of the boulder at the camp.

'Yeah,' Daniel said. 'I thought Hellfire would have at least a dozen men. But I can see only two.'

'Don't surprise me,' Lincoln said. He glanced at Billy and sneered. 'I know Hellfire. And I reckon this no-good varmint overheard my challenge and told him about it, and Hellfire couldn't resist taking it up. He's gone to Calamity to meet me and left just enough men here to guard Cooper's family.'

'Let's hope you're right.'

Lincoln snorted his assurance, then settled down. For the next ten minutes they watched the encampment.

Hellfire had holed up in Wildman's Gulch, a rocky gash in the wilderness fifteen miles north of Stark Pass. He had secured an area at the top of a slope before a sheer crag that provided a wide view of the surrounding area.

Behind the camp, under an overhang, there was a cave and, as Hellfire's men had piled wood in the entrance, presumably as a wind-break, Lincoln reckoned it was a reasonable deduction that the hostages were there.

One man was sitting by the dying remnants of a fire. Another man was patrolling back and forth with the bored indifference of someone who didn't expect anyone to approach. A third man emerged from the cave and spoke to them, then wandered back inside.

Lincoln noted that this man was the most problematic. With a secure location such as the cave to hide in, he could hold them off and, if capture were imminent, take deadly revenge on Cooper's family.

So Lincoln whispered orders to Alvin and Daniel, then backed down the slope. Bent double, he took a circuitous route around the crag that came out on the overhang.

He peered over the edge and noted he was ten yards above and fifty yards to the left of the cave, then he shuffled back from the edge. Aware now of his bearings he headed to a spot above the cave, but as he shuffled to the edge again he heard voices.

He hunkered down and listened. When he heard the voices again, he realized that they were emerging through a fissure. The fissure was thin and sheer, about three feet wide and set thirty feet from the edge. He shuffled down quietly and peered into the fissure while listening.

He could see the bottom about forty feet below and it immediately turned towards the edge then disappeared from his view, but he guessed that it tunnelled to the cave. One of voices emerging was a woman's and the other was a man's, but he couldn't make out the words.

He considered slipping down the fissure and attacking Hellfire's men from an unexpected direction, but he decided that the fissure was too difficult to traverse quietly. He shuffled to the edge of the overhang and peered over the side.

Below, the men were in the same positions as before. From his elevated position he could see the top of Daniel's hat. He looked for Alvin, who by now should have reached an outcrop, twenty yards to the right of the cave, but his deputy was well-hidden.

For the next fifteen minutes, he bided his time as he waited until one of the outlaws passed by Alvin's position and Alvin could get a drop on him. His plan was that when that man didn't return, the other outlaw would go to investigate; then Lincoln would mount his rescue attempt.

So, when the patrolling outlaw headed to the outcrop Lincoln crept to the edge, his gun drawn and ready to fire down at the camp.

The man shuffled behind the outcrop to be out of the view of the man by the fire. His hands went to his belt as he moved to squat, but then Alvin leapt out and grabbed him in a neck-hold from behind, his other hand slapping over his mouth.

The two men struggled, but the outlaw wriggled out from Alvin's grip, forcing Alvin to clip his jaw. The outlaw staggered back a pace but then righted himself and returned a blow that slammed Alvin into the outcrop. His head cracked into the solid rock and, as he slumped to the ground, the outlaw shouted a warning.

Instantly the outlaw by the fire jumped up and broke into a run, ready to repel the ambush. Within seconds he'd be out of Lincoln's sight-line, so Lincoln leapt from the overhang.

He crashed on to the outlaw's back, tumbling him to the ground, then grabbed the back of his head and hammered his forehead into the stony ground, knocking him cold.

He looked up. The other outlaw was running back to confront him; further away Daniel was running up the slope towards the cave while laying down covering fire. Lincoln added to the gunfire but when the approaching outlaw dived for cover behind a boulder Lincoln accepted his exposed position and ran for the cave. He reached it ten paces ahead of Daniel and vaulted the wooden wind-barrier in the entrance.

But running towards him from deeper within the cave was the other man and he fired on the run. Lincoln dived to the side, his leap saving him from a bullet that whined past his head and flew through the cave entrance. From behind him Daniel fired into the cave, the lead whistling past the running man to zing back and forth across the cave.

Lying on his side, Lincoln fired again but his finger twitched on an empty chamber. In desperation, he rolled to his feet and launched himself at the man. He grabbed his arm then pushed it high. The man wasted a shot into the cave roof, the shot ricocheting around them, but then the two men slammed together.

Outside the cave gunfire ripped out, but Lincoln gritted his teeth and ignored it. He pulled back his fist and slugged the man's jaw, but his opponent shrugged off the blow, then stamped down on Lincoln's foot.

In an involuntary action, Lincoln staggered back, his grip on the outlaw's arm loosening, and the man bundled Lincoln away.

Lincoln threw out a hand towards the cave wall to stop himself falling, but his foot slipped in the loose dirt and he went to his knees. When he looked up, it was to see the outlaw swing his gun down at him and steady his aim, but Daniel had vaulted the wooden barrier and he tore a slug into the man's left hip. The man staggered to the side as he fired, Daniel's shot diverting his aim. Lead whistled over Lincoln's left shoulder and cannoned into the cave wall.

As the man thrust out his right leg and stopped himself falling, Lincoln leapt to his feet and charged him. On the run, he hurled an uppercut to the man's chin that knocked his feet from under him and slammed him into the cave wall before he slid to the ground.

The man shook himself. With his hands shaking

83

he aimed his gun up at Lincoln, but Daniel took careful aim and thundered repeated gunfire into his chest, his body twitching with each blast before it lay still.

Lincoln nodded his thanks as he reloaded, but his deputy was staring over his shoulder and gesturing down. Lincoln winced and threw himself to the ground, the action saving him from a burst of gunfire that scythed over his head as it blasted in through the cave entrance.

He rolled over and came up on his belly, his gun thrust out before him, then fired wildly through the cave entrance. One shot ripped through the chest of the man running towards the cave, but he didn't wait to celebrate his victory, he peered over the wind barrier.

Down the slope, Alvin and the remaining guard were locked in a furious battle, both men rolling over each other as each tried to turn his gun on the other.

With a barked order to Daniel to cover him Lincoln vaulted the wind barrier and hurtled down the slope. He got to within five paces of the fighting twosome when Alvin's opponent slugged Alvin away. But before he could turn his gun on Alvin, Lincoln hammered a shot into the man's guts that staggered him a back a pace.

But the man righted himself and returned fire, his shot pluming into the dirt at Lincoln's feet. So this time, Lincoln nipped a shot into his neck which spun his feet from the ground before he slammed to the earth.

Then he joined Alvin. The lawmen stood poised, waiting for more trouble, but the slope returned to quietness.

Lincoln patted Alvin's shoulder and pointed down the slope. Alvin looked, then winced. Billy had taken advantage of the fighting to scurry away. Lincoln directed Alvin to chase him down. Then he headed back up the slope, gathering a torch from the dying camp-fire on the way, then paced over the wind barrier and inside.

The flames danced shadows across the cave entrance, but it enabled him to see that it was deeper than he had first thought, with the main bulk of the cave stretching away to one side. Still, he had to duck to avoid scraping his head on the roof.

With the brand held aloft and his heart hammering against what he feared he might see, he walked deeper into the cave. At the bend, he slowed, hearing subdued voices and detecting two people whispering to each other – a man and a woman.

Lincoln paced around the corner. Beyond was a wider recess, twenty yards across, which had sufficient height for Lincoln to stand upright. In the centre of the recess he saw Leah huddled beside a child. By the back wall stood a cage and in it was the manacled and hunched form of Shelton Baez.

Shelton looked up, his narrowed eyes flickering with hope.

'Is that you, Lincoln?' he asked.

'It sure is,' Lincoln said, then he turned to face Leah, but she hurled protecting arms around her child and backed away to the cave wall.

'Stay away from us,' she muttered.

'Don't worry,' Shelton said. 'He's a US Marshal, and one of the best.'

Lincoln snorted. '*The* best.'

Leah nodded. 'Then I sure am glad you're here. But is my husband all right after what Hellfire did to. . . ?'

Leah gulped and lowered her head to sob, then looked back up at Lincoln, tears streaming down her cheeks.

'Marshal Cooper was mighty upset by what happened, but he was coping when we left Stark Pass.'

'Then we're both grateful.'

Lincoln nodded, then gestured for Daniel to tend to her. He hurried across the cave to consider the cage, then tapped the bars, finding them solid. He fingered the lock.

'Where did Hellfire get this?' he asked Shelton.

'It's a cage from the railroad, perhaps for trans-porting—'

'Money, once,' Lincoln said. 'I guess he thought the idea amusing.'

'Did you . . . Did you go to . . .' Shelton gulped when Lincoln nodded. He cleared his throat. 'And was. . . ?'

'Your post was burned to the ground. I guess you've lost everything.'

Shelton glanced away. 'Yeah, everything.'

Lincoln stood back from the cage and drew his gun. He sighted the lock from various angles, but as he considered where the ricochet might land, Alvin dragged the hunched form of Billy Epstein into the cave.

Shelton's eyes flared as he struggled within his manacles.

'What's that man doing here?' he shouted.

'Helping us find you.'

'But he works for Hellfire,' Shelton murmured, lowering his voice, 'I wouldn't trust nothing that man says.'

'Hey, I heard that,' Billy shouted. 'And I wouldn't trust anything that snake says either.'

Shelton shook his fists, rattling his manacles against the side of the cage, while Billy shouted an oath at him.

'Alvin, Daniel,' Lincoln shouted, 'get Billy and the hostages outside while I free Shelton.'

Daniel helped Leah to her feet, the child throwing her arms around her neck and, with Alvin escorting the grumbling Billy, they headed to the cave entrance.

When they'd headed round the corner, Lincoln aimed at the lock, then fired. The first three shots cannoned away, but the fourth sprang the lock, letting the door fly open.

Shelton nodded his thanks. 'Hope you can do that with these manacles.'

'I will, provided you don't move while I'm firing.'

But as Lincoln sighted the first manacle Alvin

shouted a warning from the cave entrance. Lincoln turned to see his deputy sprinting round the corner and crying out that Hellfire had returned.

'I said you shouldn't have trusted Billy,' Shelton said. 'He's led you into a trap.'

Lincoln gritted his teeth on hearing this possible truth. He ran past Billy, favouring him with a harsh glare, to the cave entrance.

As Alvin had reported, down the slope, Hellfire's men had returned and were milling just out of firing range. Lincoln knelt down behind the wooden barrier. He counted at least fifteen men taking up secure positions surrounding the cave.

But then one of Hellfire's men broke off from the group and ran up the slope. Lincoln and Alvin fired at him, but the man leapt into a hollow and stayed down. Lincoln saw a thin stream of smoke plume up from his position.

Then the man himself emerged. He held a burning brand aloft. With an overhand throw he hurled the brand at the cave.

Lincoln ducked, but the brand landed on the wooden barrier which, within seconds, roared into flame. He risked leaning over to try to bat the brand away, but sustained gunfire from below forced him to dive for cover.

By then it was too late and the barrier was alight, the flames roaring up as the wind that funnelled into the cave fed the fire. Less than thirty seconds after the brand had landed the flames had spread across the cave entrance, completely cutting off their escape route.

Lincoln winced, realizing now that the barrier wasn't there to stop the wind.

This *was* a trap and Hellfire had stacked the wood in the cave entrance to burn them alive.

CHAPTER 10

With his arm thrown across his face, Lincoln braved an approach to the cave entrance, but the blistering heat forced him to hurry back.

'Hellfire,' he roared, 'you don't want to end it this way. This is just about us. Put out the fire and you can have me, but let the others go.'

He lowered his arm. Through the shimmering wall of flame he saw Hellfire stride up the slope.

'I heard promises like that sixteen years ago,' Hellfire shouted. 'They weren't true then and they aren't true now. You'll die, just like my woman died.'

Lincoln opened his mouth to shout at Hellfire, but then slapped his fist against his thigh, deciding that talking was using up the limited time he had left to find a way to escape.

He ran back into the main recess, but smoke had already filled the top half of the cave, the swirling barrier lowering even as he looked. Alvin was holding Billy by the side wall. Lincoln strode towards him, grabbed his collar and pulled him up straight.

'What kind of mad plan was this? You've got us all trapped.'

Billy coughed. 'I never expected him to do this. You got to believe me.'

Lincoln held on to Billy, then snorted. 'I guess even you aren't stupid enough to help Hellfire burn you alive.'

He threw Billy to the ground, then gathered his deputies around him.

'What . . .' Alvin said, then paused to bark out a racking cough. 'What we going to do?'

Lincoln extracted a kerchief from his pocket and waved it.

'First, put kerchiefs over your mouths to reduce the amount of smoke you breathe in. Then, there's a fissure on the top of the overhang. It leads down into this cave. Find it!'

While Alvin and Daniel headed off to explore the extremities of the cave, Billy slumped down by the wall. As he'd found a location that was a safe distance from the flames in the entrance, Lincoln ordered Leah and Mollie to lie on the ground beside him. Then he ran to the cage.

He climbed inside and fingered the manacles, finding that the bands that secured Shelton's wrist had a lock, but a short chain connected them to the cage. Lincoln directed Shelton to duck, then shot through the chains.

The freed Shelton grunted his approval while slapping Lincoln's back. When they'd slipped out of the cage Alvin and Daniel were already pointing. Lincoln followed the direction of their pointing to see that the smoke was curling towards the back of the cave, suggesting that the fissure was there, drawing the smoke in that direction.

But the smoke had already filled the cave down to head level. Even with the kerchief over his mouth Lincoln had to fight down the urge to cough with every breath.

With the urgency for getting out of the cave growing with every passing second, the group needed no encouragement to trail from the cave and down the short tunnel at the back.

In the growing darkness they squeezed over a clutter of boulders and down a short incline. Then the light-level grew until they stood below the fissure. It was a vertical chimney, about forty feet high, but with handholds and several ledges.

Lincoln directed Daniel to help Leah climb and Alvin to carry the child. Leah objected but a shake of the head from Lincoln encouraged her to relent.

But then, behind him, Shelton screeched. Lincoln turned to see that Billy had jumped him and the two men were struggling on the ground. Each man had his hands planted on the other's neck and was trying to squeeze and wrestle the other man on to his back.

Lincoln ordered Alvin and Leah to begin the ascent, then swirled round and grabbed Billy's shoulder. He pulled him away, but that only gave Shelton enough room to firm his footing and launch another attack on Billy. So, Lincoln grabbed Shelton's collar and pulled him back.

With the two men held at arm's length, he glared at each of them in turn.

'We got just a few minutes to get out of here,' he muttered. 'Whatever this is about can wait.'

Billy launched a fist at Shelton but it fell well short and Shelton directed a kick at Billy, which also fell short. Even when Lincoln shook them the men continued to struggle. But then the smoke funnelling out through the fissure dragged a painful burst of coughing from both of them they nodded reluctantly and backed away from each other.

Lincoln snorted his disgust for them, then directed Shelton to climb the fissure after Daniel. He held Billy back and only let him climb when Shelton was a good ten feet above his head. Then Lincoln started climbing.

The fissure was thin, but this enabled Lincoln to plant a hand on either side and, with his back braced, head upward.

One by the one they emerged on to the ground above, then rolled away from the smoke pouring out of the fissure. Lincoln clambered out last. Like the others, he dragged away his kerchief and lay on his back, staring at the sky while dragging in long breaths.

But around him the others were coughing loudly and Lincoln rolled to his knees.

'We all want to get the smoke out of our lungs,' he said, 'but do it quietly. Hellfire might hear us.'

He was answered with several nods and a few suppressed coughs. Then, on his belly, he shuffled to the edge of the overhang and peered over.

The smoke pluming from the wooden barrier obscured his vision. But below him he could see the shimmering outlines of Hellfire and his men, who were milling before the cave entrance.

He debated ambushing them, but a glance over his shoulder at his deputies, who were still lying on their backs with their chests heaving, convinced him that they were in no shape to mount an effective assault.

Though their horses were only fifty yards away from the cave Lincoln reckoned they probably couldn't get to them. But from the intensity of the heat rippling up from the cave entrance, Lincoln judged that the fire would burn for another hour, and that gave them enough time to get some distance away from Hellfire.

But even then, Stark Pass was fifteen miles away; Calamity was ten miles distant.

He turned, but at that moment, Billy was dragging himself to his feet. Then he launched himself at Shelton.

Lincoln winced and gestured at them to stop fighting, but both men ignored him and Alvin had his back to him as he helped Leah and Mollie to crawl away from the fissure. Daniel was on his back, gasping air.

Lincoln rolled to his feet and, keeping his head down, ran towards them. Both men were now slugging it out with round-armed blows and much kicking of dirt. Such a commotion had to attract Hellfire's attention before long.

But then Billy dragged himself free of Shelton's clutches and delivered a solid punch that knocked his opponent towards the opening of the deep fissure. Shelton teetered on the edge, his arms wheeling as he fought for balance.

Billy rolled his shoulders and charged him, aiming to push him over the edge, but at the last second, Shelton half-slipped, half-hurled himself to the side to land on his belly with his feet dangling over the edge.

Billy jabbed in a heel, trying to halt his progress, but he skidded past Shelton and tumbled into the hole. With an echoing shriek, he clattered down it, his shrieking dying as he crashed to the bottom.

A huge puff of smoke billowed up as Shelton slipped another foot down the hole. He tore his fingers into the dirt as he searched for purchase, but he continued to slip. Inch by inexorable inch he slid away. But Lincoln was running at full tilt: he threw himself to the ground and skidded on his belly to grab Shelton's clawing hand as it slipped from view.

They locked hands, Shelton's body dangling above the smoky void. Lincoln peered down, seeing Billy lying at the bottom, his neck presenting a sharp angle. But then the smoke rolled over him and Shelton's weight and the lack of purchase on the ground dragged Lincoln towards the edge.

Lincoln planted his elbows wide but Shelton's weight still dragged him over the ground. He scrambled his legs but that only speeded his movement. But then arms wrapped around his chest and stopped him. He was just nodding his thanks to Daniel when he realized the hands were Leah's.

'Be careful,' he urged. 'I'm heavier than you are.'

'Then don't struggle,' she grunted. 'Daniel's coming. I'll hold you until then.'

Lincoln nodded. Within moments another pair of hands landed on his back and dragged him and Shelton out and on to solid ground.

They lay a moment, gasping, but Lincoln directed them to get away from the hole and draw breath behind a heap of boulders that lay fifty yards from the fissure, a safe distance from the edge of the overhang.

Everyone nodded their approval and scurried to safety. Lincoln expected that the combination of the smoke filtering out through the fissure and Billy's shriek would alert Hellfire and he darted his gaze between the overhang and the approaches from either side. But after ten minutes Hellfire still hadn't come to investigate and Lincoln started to plan their next action.

As he considered his gaze kept returning to Shelton, whose prolonged looks encouraged Lincoln to shuffle to his side.

'What's wrong?' Shelton asked.

'I'm just wondering,' Lincoln said, 'if I can trust you.'

'Did I need a good reason to fight that snake?'

'I guess not, but once I get us out of this, I'll want to know what you were fighting about.'

Shelton sighed. 'That mean you don't know already?'

Lincoln considered Shelton, then shrugged. 'I reckon that sixteen years ago Billy was either a bad lawman or he was trying to help Hellfire get away. But if you got something else to tell me, it'd be better for you if you just volunteered it.'

Shelton stared at the ground between his feet, his uncertain gaze suggesting he was considering how much Lincoln already knew.

Then he shrugged. 'I guess I've wanted to tell someone about this for years.' Shelton took a deep breath. 'Amidst all the shooting and confusion, I escaped and found the fifty thousand dollars. I figured Billy was planning to steal it and would come back for it later, so I hid it, figuring that when I found someone I could trust, I'd give it to them. But what with having to make a fresh start after the fire, I got to thinking . . .'

'And Billy?'

'He always reckoned I'd found it, but he couldn't prove nothing.'

Lincoln nodded. 'I can't say how bad that is for you.'

Shelton looked skyward, his eyes watering. 'It's already worse than you can imagine. That secret has cost me everything.'

'I'm here,' Harvey shouted, his voice echoing down Calamity's main road. 'I've come here to see you.'

He waited – not that he expected an immediate answer. He had tried to find the woman's footprints, but had found no more signs of her passage.

But when she'd disappeared she had been heading in the general direction of Calamity, and Harvey couldn't believe she would go anywhere else but here. Or that Shelton hadn't meant him to do anything other than find this woman when he had directed him to give 'her' this box.

After he had freed the ropes from his hands he had tried to prise open the box, but a clasp held the lid firm. A keyhole confirmed that he'd have to find the key or break it open to get inside.

'I'm here,' he shouted, but his voice echoed back to him from the abandoned buildings.

There wasn't much to the town, just two rows of standing buildings, so it took Harvey only five minutes to roam the length of the main road. Then he explored the buildings. Dirt and dust had accumulated in their shells, but in each he found no sign that anyone had been through here.

And certainly no sign that anyone lived here.

Sightings of a ghost in Calamity had been common and had helped to keep people away, but if someone had been living here, and perhaps fuelling those ghost rumours, they needed a base.

But none of the buildings was a likely place for anyone to live in.

Only when he reached the station did he find recent horse-prints. But as far as he could tell the riders had just stopped beside the station, then moved on. He didn't think they had anything to do with the woman.

'I'm Harvey Baez,' he shouted, but his voice wasn't much louder than the wind that swirled and whined between the buildings. 'Shelton sent me. Something terrible has happened to him. Hellfire kidnapped him and I want to save him. And I think you can help me.'

Harvey stood on the platform, hoping that whatever bond Shelton felt for this woman was mutual, but when he heard no answer, he paraded around on the spot, waving the box above his head.

'Shelton told me to find you and give you this. I've got no idea what it is or what it means, but it's important that you get it.'

Harvey knelt and placed the box on the edge of the platform, then turned. Fired by his desire to resolve the mystery of who she was and what she wanted, he investigated the town again, avoiding even looking towards the station.

This time his thorough investigation discovered many places where someone could hide: under the boardwalk, beneath the saloon, amidst the ruined remnants of the disintegrating stable.

But aside from rodents nobody had lived in any of these places. And when he returned to the station the box was still where he'd left it.

'I know you're hiding here somewhere,' Harvey shouted, picking up the box and holding it aloft. 'But I'm not leaving until you see me. I just hope you don't wait long. Because I reckon you're the only person who can save Shelton's life.'

Harvey wandered back down the road. He didn't expect a quick answer, but to his surprise he heard a holler from behind. He swirled round to see who had spoken, but the town was deserted.

But then he realized that the holler had come from out of town, that riders were heading down the side of the railtracks.

And after all the bad luck of the last few hours Harvey had no doubt that Hellfire was amongst those men.

Lincoln sought his deputies' views as to their next action.

Daniel thought Calamity was a good place to hole up. Alvin reckoned they should go to Stark Pass, as they could ensure Leah's and Mollie's safety there.

Lincoln decided to take the best parts of both plans. He directed Alvin to head to Stark Pass and fetch help, while he led the rest on a direct route to Calamity.

They walked for an hour with Daniel trailing behind and swiping away the obvious signs of their trail. They covered several miles, by which time Lincoln judged that Hellfire would have been able to get into the cave and discover that they had escaped.

And it was only a matter of time before he came after them.

And sure enough, when the weary group reached the edge of an incline, two miles from Calamity, from where they could see the rail tracks below, a troop of men rode into view, following the tracks.

These men didn't include Hellfire, but they were searching for them and, from the way they repeatedly glanced at the ground, Lincoln reckoned they had picked up a trail, but had now lost it.

But then one of the riders stopped, peered at the ground, and drew the others around him. They milled, but then the lead man gesticulated and two men hurried along the tracks while another two peeled off and headed up the slope.

Lincoln slipped back from the edge and joined Daniel while Shelton, Leah and Mollie sat beside a boulder.

'They picked up a trail,' Daniel said, 'but it ain't ours.'

'No argument there, but that won't matter if they accidentally find us.'

Daniel nodded, and after a short debate they agreed upon the route that the men would take when they reached the top of the slope. As that route headed between two large sentinel rocks, Lincoln and Daniel hurried there, then climbed up on either side of the rocks to lie on their tops.

Lincoln lay flat to the rock and listened to the clop of the men's horses as they approached them. He exchanged gestures with Alvin on the other rock, then shuffled to the edge and peered over the side. The men were riding towards them. Within seconds they'd be directly below.

Lincoln stood, still keeping back to ensure they wouldn't be able to see him. Then, on the count of three, he and Alvin leapt from the rocks.

Lincoln slammed on to the right-hand rider's shoulders, knocking him from his horse. He was aware of Daniel also unseating his target, but then the two men hit the ground and rolled over, their limbs entangled.

Lincoln's opponent struggled out from under him, but Lincoln's right cross to the chin knocked him back on his haunches and his second blow to the cheek pole-axed him.

Daniel had fallen awkwardly and his opponent had rolled clear. That man gained his footing first and, as Lincoln turned to them, he slugged Daniel's jaw, crashing him on to his back.

Lincoln ran to him, aiming to silently subdue him, but when the man drew his gun and aimed it down at the sprawling Daniel, Lincoln had no choice but to blast lead into his back, sending him sprawling.

As the gunfire echoes faded to silence Lincoln confirmed that the man was dead; he dragged Daniel to his feet and ordered him to secure the horses. Then he ran to the edge of the slope, hanging on to the hope that the group below wouldn't interpret the gunfire as anything more than their colleagues' exuberance.

But below, the group exchanged a set of barked orders, then trooped towards the slope and hurried up it.

Lincoln watched them, assuring himself that they were intent on attacking them, then he rolled back from the edge. But it was to see that Daniel and Shelton had rounded up only one of the horses. The other horse was galloping away and heading towards the edge of the slope, throwing up its heels in a way that suggested they wouldn't capture it in the minute or so they had before the men found them.

As Shelton joined him Lincoln glanced around, searching for the best place to make their stand.

'We can still make it to Calamity,' Shelton said. 'And make a stand there.'

'We could,' Lincoln said. 'But we only got one horse and it ain't carrying all of us.'

Shelton stood tall and patted the gun he'd taken off the unconscious outlaw.

'It will if I stay behind.'

Lincoln didn't look at him or waste a second considering the offer.

'You ain't doing that.'

'Just get the child and the woman to safety and forget about me.'

'Shelton, I wouldn't be a lawman if I did that.'

'Then just go anyhow. I stole and I'll pay the price for that later, but I'd sooner pay for it here, getting revenge on the men who killed ... on these men.'

Lincoln glared hard at Shelton, but as Shelton returned an encouraging nod he patted his back, then turned away before he could persuade himself this was a bad idea. He mounted the horse. Alvin slipped in behind him, then reached down to help Leah and the child up to sit on his lap.

With so much weight, the horse wouldn't be able to carry them far, but Calamity was less than two miles away.

'What's Shelton doing?' Daniel asked.

'He ain't coming,' Lincoln murmured as he headed to the top of the slope.

As Daniel murmured in understanding the riders swung round to head through the sentinel rocks. So, picking their route gingerly, they arced down the slope towards the tracks. Lincoln glanced over his shoulder as the rocks disappeared from view, but Shelton had already taken cover.

Still, he gave a silent salute, then concentrated on finding a safe route down to the railroad tracks.

Then behind them gunfire ripped out, the sounds echoing back and forth between the high rocks. It was sustained and ferocious, the blasts seemingly reporting from many directions as Shelton gave the men a battle. Lincoln firmed his jaw and hurried on.

But when they reached ground level and the side of the tracks, the gunfire spluttered to silence.

Lincoln winced, but still he encouraged the horse to achieve the fastest speed it could and, at a fair trot, they headed down the side of the tracks towards Calamity. He repeatedly glanced back, looking for the moment when the men worked out where they had gone and headed after them, but they got closer and closer to Calamity with still no sign of pursuit.

The sun was edging towards the horizon, casting a long shadow before them as they swung round to head down the main road. But then Lincoln saw a plume of dust rising beyond the railtracks. Within seconds it resolved into the forms of the pursuing riders.

Lincoln slowed to search for the best place to mount their defence when Hellfire's men did arrive. They trotted past the station and Lincoln drew his horse to a halt beside the saloon, the hard-pressed steed rearing as Lincoln glanced over his shoulder.

The pursuers *were* closing on them, now just a mile back. But that wasn't the worst of their problems.

There, in the centre of the road, was the very cage in which Hellfire had previously imprisoned Shelton.

'Why is that here?' Alvin shouted.

'Because,' Lincoln murmured, 'Hellfire's already here.'

CHAPTER 11

From all around, gunfire exploded – from the ruined wreckage of the stable, from the store, from both ends of the road.

Lincoln yanked the reins to the side, aiming to gallop out of town, but a slug thudded into the horse's flank and forced it to stumble. With no choice, Lincoln jumped from the saddle and, along with Alvin, they stood on either side of Leah and Mollie, but the shooting was relentless, the slugs whining all around them.

So they ran to the only place from where gunfire wasn't coming, the saloon. But as they clattered on to the boardwalk two men bobbed up to fire at them through the broken windows.

Lincoln and Alvin had already committed themselves to seeking cover here, so Lincoln charged through the doorway, kicking open the only batwing, while Alvin leapt through the right-hand window. Lincoln danced to the side and blasted the man by the left-hand window, knocking him off his feet and back through the window to land on the boardwalk outside.

On the run, Alvin tore gunfire into the second man, spinning him around to slam into the wall and slide to the floor. Then they covered Leah and the child as they hurried in after them.

As quickly as possible Lincoln positioned Leah and Mollie behind the remnants of the bar, then he hunkered down beside the door. He peered outside.

Gunfire still peppered the saloon wall sporadically, but from it Lincoln judged the number of men they were facing. By his estimate at least a dozen men had taken over Calamity.

Groups had stationed themselves at the edge of the road in both directions and others fired around the sides of the stable and the store. In the shell of the building opposite another group of had men congregated.

But as yet he hadn't located Hellfire.

'Hellfire,' he shouted, 'attacking a US marshal is a big mistake.'

'I got nothing to say to you, Lincoln Hawk,' a voice shouted from the town store.

Lincoln snorted on recognizing Hellfire's voice.

'And neither are you getting any closer to that fifty thousand dollars.'

'And I reckon I am. Somebody knows where it is and I reckon you're that somebody.'

Lincoln searched for another taunt, but then decided to remain quiet. He'd done the more important thing and located him.

'Alvin,' he said, looking over his shoulder,

'secure the back. Leah, you stay where you are. Mollie, you go to sleep.'

Presently three riders emerged from the gathering gloom to gallop into town. Lincoln relayed this information to Alvin, not mentioning that these were the men who had overcome Shelton. Although, as their numbers had reduced considerably, Shelton had clearly given better than he'd received.

These men dismounted fifty yards from the saloon as, from across the road, Hellfire's men used the distraction to edge out on to the road, but Lincoln sprayed wild gunfire at them and forced them to dive for cover.

'If that's the best they can do,' Lincoln said, hurrying the last man into cover with a final gunshot, 'we will prevail.'

'Yeah,' Alvin said with a wink from his position at the back door. 'These men ain't that impressive.'

Lincoln settled down beside the window, unable to suppress a smile as he prepared for a short siege.

Daniel had headed to Stark Pass and although that town was five miles further away than Calamity, his deputy had been travelling alone and so should have been able to reach there by now. And that meant a posse should be coming here to rescue them before long. Lincoln had only to hold out until then.

To ensure Hellfire's men didn't feel confident and storm the saloon, Lincoln provided sporadic gunfire that peppered the surrounding buildings, but as none of the men showed themselves he didn't hit anyone.

That didn't concern Lincoln. Every minute that he kept them at bay was another minute less that they had to wait for the posse. But time passed slowly as the cage in the middle of the road caught the sun's last rays and darkness descended. But the moon was nearly full and provided sufficient light to give Lincoln a decent view of the road.

At the back door Alvin quietly kept look-out and Leah murmured a low and soothing lullaby to her daughter.

But just as Lincoln detected a growing level of confidence in himself that they could last out, he heard a scrambling, as of someone clambering over the roof. He looked up, but the roof covered only half of the saloon, and the part that was covered didn't look strong enough to support a bird, never mind a man.

But he heard the scrambling again.

Lincoln glanced at Alvin, who had cocked his head to the side trying to identify from where the sound was coming, but it was Leah who raised a hand to attract Lincoln's attention, then she pointed downwards.

Lincoln glanced at the floor, then nodded, realizing that she was right and that somebody was crawling about *under* the saloon. Everyone's gaze centred on a hole in the floor behind the bar, then Leah screamed and rocked back as a man climbed out of that hole.

'Reach,' Lincoln muttered, sighting the man down the barrel of his gun.

The man screeched and hurled his hands aloft, his whole body shaking with suppressed fear and causing Lincoln to flinch back when he realized that the man was only a boy, perhaps fourteen or fifteen. He held a box aloft in a raised hand and his eyes were wide and scared.

'Now, son,' Lincoln said, 'you sure you're old enough to be one of Hellfire's hired guns?'

'I ain't no hired gun, sir. I'm Harvey, Harvey Baez. I was hiding and I heard you talking and my uncle always said I should trust Marshal Lincoln Hawk.'

'Your uncle is a wise man. Is he. . . ?'

'Shelton Baez,' Harvey murmured.

Lincoln gritted his teeth to suppress a wince.

'I understand. Now lower your hands and join Leah. You're in no danger while you're with me.'

Harvey gave a nervous nod, then dropped his hands to his side.

'I trust you,' he said as he joined Leah, 'but you got to get that Hellfire. He took my uncle and I reckon he might have killed him.'

Lincoln glanced at Alvin, who looked away, then at Leah, who lowered her head.

'Perhaps when this is over we can find out what happened to him.'

To avoid the uncomfortable subject, Lincoln hunkered down beside the door and fired two quick shots at the store opposite, but his enticing firing couldn't persuade Hellfire to return fire and, with only limited ammunition, Lincoln desisted.

Within the saloon everyone remained calm. Lincoln was pleased to hear that despite the occasional scare Leah continued to sing to Mollie, but Harvey was staring at the man Alvin had shot when they'd first come into the saloon. Then he shuffled across the saloon and collected the man's gun.

'You sure you're safe with that gun, son?' Lincoln asked.

Harvey headed back across the saloon, then sat against the bar with the gun cradled in his lap.

'I reckon I can aim and fire.' He leaned back to place the box on the bar, then hefted the weapon. 'Might not hit anything, but it might help.'

'It might.' Lincoln watched Harvey's hand shake and, to try to take his mind off the fear the young man was clearly feeling, he pointed at the box on the bar. 'What's in the box?'

Harvey glanced at the box and flinched, as if he were noticing it for the first time.

'My uncle gave it to me just before ... just before Hellfire took him. I have to give it to ... to someone.'

'And who is that *someone*?'

Harvey's eyes glazed. 'I don't know for sure. I got me an idea who he meant, but she can't be ... I don't for sure, just that I had to give it to her, but he never said who *her* was.'

'And you don't know what's in the box?'

'I don't, sir. It's locked and I don't have the key.'

Lincoln raised his eyebrows. 'You mind if I open it for you?'

Harvey took the box from the bar and slid it across the saloon floor. It stopped four feet short of Lincoln, but, with one eye closed, Lincoln sighted the box then blasted the clasp away.

The force tumbled the box end over end, but when it came to a halt, the lid had opened. Lincoln glanced through the window to check nobody from outside could see him move then crawled to the box and grabbed it. He returned to the window and looked inside.

Aside from a folded slip of paper the box was empty. With his brow furrowed Lincoln removed the paper and read it, then snorted.

'One bag of corn,' he read, 'a side of salted beef, two . . .'

'A list of provisions,' Harvey murmured.

'Yeah.' Lincoln glanced at Harvey. 'Is this some kind of joke?'

'No,' Harvey blurted, 'this is what Shelton gave me to give to her.'

'The list,' Alvin said, 'or the provisions?'

'What you thinking?' Lincoln asked, turning to his deputy.

'Shelton was a trading man. Perhaps he didn't want to disappoint a customer.'

Alvin murmured a laugh, but Lincoln just flashed him a glare that silenced his good humour, then shook his head.

'There's something I'm not seeing here.'

Lincoln read the list again, but however he looked at it, the list was just a list of food and enough to keep one person fed for at least a month. He held the list up to the window but there was no more writing on it. He fingered the box, peering at the plain sides, but there was nothing else to the box.

If Shelton had stolen the $50,000, a last note like this ought to provide a clue as to its location, but Lincoln couldn't see that this was anything other than a list of provisions. He placed the note back in the box and kicked it across the floor to Harvey, who looked at the note, then closed his eyes and sighed.

'This must be wrong,' he whispered.

'What were you expecting?'

Harvey lowered his head. 'I . . . I . . . I don't know.'

Lincoln stared at Harvey, assuming that his shaking hands meant he had expected something else, but as he considered how he could push him for more details without worrying him, Alvin raised a hand.

'Lincoln,' he said from the back door, 'you'd better come and see this. They're moving into position. And I reckon this time they're planning to take us.'

Lincoln joined Alvin to peer out through the back door, seeing a man scurrying through the gloom to hide in a hollow. Then, through the front window, he saw several men hurrying to new positions.

He had a deputy, a scared woman and child, and a frightened young man, who, from the loose way he held his gun, was in greater danger of shooting off his own foot than killing any of Hellfire's men.

Hellfire had at least a dozen men, and they were only the ones Lincoln had seen. And, from the steady way they edged forward, each time under covering gunfire, they had a plan to secure the best strategic positions around the saloon.

'Daniel will be here with that posse soon,' Lincoln announced. 'We just need to hang on for a little while longer.'

He glanced at Harvey, who was cowering at the corner of the bar, then at Leah, who had grabbed a length of wood, the only weapon she could find. She'd tucked Mollie behind the bar. Then he peered out into the road, waiting until Hellfire's men were close enough to present tempting targets.

But he didn't have to wait long.

They hollered orders to each other, more to instil fear than to organize themselves. Then a wave of men charged out into the road, heading straight for the saloon in an all-out assault, every man firing on the run.

Lincoln returned fire, catching one man in a high shot that wheeled him to the ground and a second man with a low shot that cut his legs from under him. But the rest redoubled their firing and, with the last shards of glass from the window cascading around him, Lincoln had to duck.

Lincoln waited for a brief lull, then bobbed up. But he was shocked to find the road was clear, every man presumably having gained cover nearer to the saloon. Then, at the back exit, Alvin fired frantically through the door. And Lincoln realized that the run was just a ruse to get men around the back of the saloon and launch their assault from there.

Gunfire ripped through the back door, forcing Alvin to retreat, but he kept firing outside. Then a man jumped into the doorway, Alvin ripped a slug into his chest, but a second man vaulted over this man's tumbling body, then dived to the floor.

Alvin's shot scythed over the man's head. But Lincoln took longer aim and slammed lead into the man's side, whirling him away. His second shot thudded into his body.

But, with a last, dying finger-twitch, the man blasted a slug up into Alvin. The shot hit him high, blood flying as it ripped through his shoulder.

Alvin staggered back, but as his free hand rose to clutch his wound, three men charged through the door and peppered a vast explosion of gunfire across the saloon, which forced Lincoln to dive for cover behind a table.

He saw Alvin go down in a hail of gunfire, bullets tearing into his chest as he staggered backwards. But Lincoln gained cover, then discovered that he wasn't their target. The group covered one man who ran to the bar and grabbed Leah, batting the plank from her hands before she'd been able to get in a single retaliatory blow. A second man scooped up Mollie.

Harvey glanced up at the end of the bar, but then dived for cover. When Lincoln bobbed up the leading man turned Leah to face him, using her body as a human shield. Then they backed away to the door and outside. The moment they'd slipped through the door Lincoln hurried across the room, but then a loud explosion of gunfire ripped out at the front of the saloon.

Lincoln wavered for a moment then fast-crawled to the window to see two riders galloping into town, the leading man firing to left and right. Lincoln breathed a sigh of relief on seeing that it was Daniel with Marshal Cooper in tow. He laid down a burst of covering gunfire that forced Hellfire's men to stay down.

Daniel and Cooper dismounted. Daniel was at the back, but as he covered Cooper two of Hellfire's men dared to leap out from the stable. Lincoln fired at the first man, wheeling him to the ground, but the second man dropped to lie on his belly and delivered a slug to the guts that wheeled Daniel on to the boardwalk.

Lincoln hammered two shots into this man, rolling him on to his back, as Cooper slid to a halt in the saloon doorway. Then he dashed back and, with Lincoln covering him, helped Daniel into the saloon.

'Sure am glad to see you,' Lincoln said, grabbing Daniel's shoulder and helping Cooper drag him inside.

'Almost didn't make it,' Daniel said, clutching his guts as Lincoln propped him up against the wall beside the door. 'But I said I'd come.'

Lincoln glanced at the red flood cascading over Daniel's clawed hands, then smiled and patted his shoulder.

116

'We'll be fine now you're here.'

Daniel nodded, then slumped to lie on his side. Lincoln watched him, seeing a bubble of blood ripple over his lips, his breathing too shallow to remove it, then he swirled round to face Cooper.

'Where's the rest?' he snapped.

'You just got me,' Cooper said. He glanced at the dying deputy, then at Alvin's body lying beside the back exit. He considered Harvey beside the bar, then turned back to Lincoln. 'I'm a lawman and lawmen are best suited to deal with the likes of Hellfire. I don't waste the lives of my townsfolk.'

'But you got the right to raise a posse.'

'Don't tell me what I can do.' Cooper peered around. 'Now, where's Leah?'

Lincoln sighed. 'If you'd got here two minutes earlier, she'd have been safe behind the bar, but Hellfire's men ambushed me and took her.'

'And you just let them?'

Lincoln threw his hands wide, signifying the ruined saloon and the rest of Calamity.

'Unless you hadn't noticed, I'm heavily outnumbered here.'

'And you should have thought of that before you tried your ridiculous rescue attempt. Rescuing her was my job.'

Lincoln gestured to the outside. 'Then I'd be most obliged to hear your idea of how we get her back.'

'I've done plenty of thinking.' Cooper watched Lincoln and when Lincoln edged his gun through the window he swung his gun round to aim it at

Lincoln's side. 'And I have to hand you over.'

'Watch out,' Harvey shouted from the side of the bar, but Lincoln merely glanced at Cooper from the corner of his eye.

'Like Harvey said – take that gun off me, Cooper.'

Cooper glanced at Harvey, who had swung his gun up to aim at his back. 'And take that gun off me, boy. The way it's shaking, I doubt you could hit me.'

'I can try,' Harvey grunted.

'Harvey, don't shoot a lawman,' Lincoln said. 'Cooper will put down his gun.'

Harvey shuffled the gun into his grip, but then, with a sad shake of the head, lowered it and slapped it on to the bar.

'But I'm still not putting down my gun,' Cooper muttered. 'I promised Hellfire I'd hand you over. And I will.'

Lincoln peered down the barrel of Cooper's gun, then turned to sight the heap of barrels across the road.

'I couldn't decide before whether you were yellow-bellied or incompetent. But I never thought you were corrupt.'

'I got no choice. I can't let my family die.'

Lincoln glanced at Cooper from the corner of his eye, then drew his gun back through the window, but he held it high and away from Cooper.

'They're dead already – that's the basis you work on. The moment Hellfire captured them, you got nothing to lose by doing your duty. And he won't let them go if you hand me over.'

'You can't know that.' Cooper gestured upwards with his gun. 'Now, stand up.'

Lincoln stood and took a steady pace towards Cooper.

'I know Hellfire. He's cruel. He enjoys seeing people suffer. And you're suffering. If you hand me over, he'll still kill you and your family.'

'I have to take that chance. We're lawmen. We know the risks. My family aren't.' Cooper stood back and gestured for Lincoln to drop his gun and head to the door. 'But I'll give you this – once I've handed you over, if I get out this alive I'll turn in my star and take the consequences.'

Lincoln let his gun fall from his fingers. 'You'll swing.'

'If I do, I do, but it'll be worth it if Leah and Mollie live.'

Lincoln took long and deliberate paces towards the door, but stopped one pace away and glanced at Cooper over his shoulder.

'And what will it be like for them, living with the knowledge of what you did?'

'At least they'll be alive to worry about it.'

'There are worse things than death.'

'Tell that to my daughter.' Cooper pushed Lincoln through the door.

CHAPTER 12

'Lincoln Hawk,' Hellfire said, pacing across the road towards the saloon with his men flanking him, 'I've waited for this moment.'

On the edge of the crumbling boardwalk, Lincoln wheeled to a halt and stood with his legs planted wide.

'Cooper,' he muttered, glancing over his shoulder, 'there's still time to do the right thing.'

Inside the saloon, Cooper grabbed Harvey's arm and dragged him outside, then kicked Lincoln forwards.

'I've done what you asked, Hellfire,' he shouted. 'Now, free my family like you promised.'

'I guess you've completed on your side of the bargain.' Hellfire clicked his fingers and Burl dragged Leah out from the alley beside the saloon. He pushed her forward.

Leah stared in open-mouthed shock at Lincoln, but Cooper ran down the road towards her. She shook herself, then held her arms out for Cooper and her to embrace.

Then Cooper bent and picked up Mollie and the three hugged with their heads bowed.

Leah looked up and shared eye contact with Lincoln, but Burl broke up the group and pushed Cooper, then Leah and Mollie towards the saloon. He collected Harvey, and this time none of them looked at Lincoln as they trooped inside, leaving Lincoln standing alone before Hellfire.

'You enjoy seeing that family reunited?' Hellfire asked as he paraded back and forth before Lincoln.

Lincoln folded his arms and stood with one leg slightly bent, feigning a casual attitude as he searched for the right moment to launch an assault on Hellfire.

'Of course.'

'Then that'll fortify you against what's coming.'

Hellfire chuckled and maintained the chuckle long after any real humour would have died. His false good mood dragged an echoing snort of laughter from his men.

Hellfire directed Burl to go behind Lincoln. Then rough hands grabbed him from behind. Lincoln struggled, but a second set of hands grabbed him and pulled him back.

While rubbing his hands with barely suppressed glee, Hellfire ordered two of his largest men to pummel Lincoln. Neither man needed any encouragement to plough into him. The first man launched a flurry of short blows to Lincoln's guts, then round-armed blows to his face that rocked his head one way, then the other.

Lincoln rolled with the punches, limiting their damage and hoping the men would tire themselves out.

But if they were capable of tiring, they took their time.

Time ceased to have meaning as Lincoln's world contracted to the systematic blows he was receiving. He ebbed on the edge of consciousness and might have passed out because he suddenly realized that the blows had stopped and the pressure holding his arms had receded.

Taking this as his chance, Lincoln lurched forward, ready to make a run for Hellfire. But the blows had been worse than he expected and instead of the flat-out charge he expected, he staggered two paces then fell to his knees.

Hellfire laughed and kicked out, the toe of his boot connecting with Lincoln's chin and cracking his head back.

Darkness descended on Lincoln, but only for a moment.

Hands grabbed his arms and pulled them high. Then they wrapped ropes around his wrists. He struggled, but he had only enough strength to produce an ineffectual wriggle.

Then his arms pulled taut, the muscles creaking with the strain and shocking him to full awareness. He shook his head, freeing the blood from his eyes to see the dirt was only inches from his face.

Then the dirt moved, his cheek rasping along the ground. He raised his head, but still he moved.

Then he realized what was happening.

Hellfire's men had tied him to a horse and Burl was dragging him down the road.

Luckily, the short road was solid dirt with few stones, but Burl turned at the station, then trotted back down the road. On either side of the road Hellfire's men lined up to cheer Burl on as Lincoln ripped and bounced along the ground between them.

But Burl turned and headed past them for a second pass, then a third, and a fourth.

However much Lincoln bunched his arms, he couldn't relieve the continuous strain and the clothes on his back must have worn through because by the fifth passage, every jar tore his skin.

But then Burl stopped and someone ripped through the rope.

Lincoln lay on his back, enjoying the relief for his strained shoulder muscles, but Burl dismounted and began a persistent kicking of Lincoln's ribs that forced him to roll away then stagger to his feet.

He tried to stand upright and face Hellfire but he could only stand stooped, his arms hanging slackly before him.

'You ready to talk, Lincoln?' Hellfire asked, as he swaggered up to Lincoln.

Hellfire lifted Lincoln's head by the hair and slapped his face one way then the other, then delivered a sharp uppercut that crashed Lincoln on to his back. As Lincoln floundered Hellfire kicked out, crunching his boot into Lincoln's ribs and sending him rolling.

But when Lincoln came to a halt, he shuffled round to kneel and glared up at Hellfire.

'Is that the best you can do?' he grunted through his torn lips.

'No, it ain't,' Hellfire murmured, drawing back his boot. 'I've only just started on you.'

It was long into the night when Hellfire's men ran out of ways to pummel Lincoln.

Early in his ordeal Lincoln had gathered that Hellfire didn't want to actually kill him, although he presumed that that was only because he was saving him until he learnt whether he knew anything about the location of the missing money. After which, he'd kill him.

So, while he waited for an opportunity to retaliate, his only choice was to endure the punishment and hope he still had the strength afterwards to do something.

When they did finally relent they dragged him into the centre of the road, threw him into the cage, locked it, and paraded around it.

On his knees, Lincoln shuffled to the front and peered at Hellfire through the bars.

'You had enough, Hellfire?' he grunted.

'Nope,' Hellfire said. 'But are you ready to tell me what you know about the fifty thousand dollars?'

'It's long gone.'

'And if that's the answer, you're looking at death.'

'Why? I spared your life sixteen years ago.'

'You did, but not my woman's life,' Hellfire roared, his blemish reddening as he snorted his breath through his nostrils.

Slowly, he calmed and considered Lincoln, his head cocked to one side as he appeared to await a response. But Lincoln didn't give him the satisfaction and just returned his stare.

So Hellfire gestured to Burl, who, along with three other men, headed into the collapsed stable. They returned with their arms loaded with wood and piled it around the base of the cage, then returned to the stable to collect more.

'What you doing?' Lincoln asked.

'You die at sun-up,' Hellfire said, 'just like Adele died.'

Hellfire watched his men pile wood around the cage, then headed into the saloon, but Lincoln ignored him and looked to the saloon window.

Marshal Cooper was looking at him and Lincoln fixed him with his firm gaze. With just his eyes, he implored the lawman to accept that Hellfire would kill everyone after he'd killed him.

But Cooper met his gaze for only the briefest of moments, then turned away from the window, leaving Lincoln to watch Burl pile even more wood around the cage.

Hunched at the end of the bar, Harvey watched Hellfire stride into the saloon. He shivered.

The last few hours had been terrible as he tried and failed to overcome his shame at his lack of action during Hellfire's ambush. He had been too terrified to act when Hellfire had ambushed the trading post, and gut-wrenching fear had paralysed him when Marshal Cooper had turned on Lincoln.

And now he was too scared to do anything but sit quietly and hope Hellfire didn't notice him.

And worse, he could see no way to redeem himself.

He watched as Hellfire's gaze roved around the saloon. He tensed as it passed over him, but if Hellfire recognized him as the person he'd trapped in the burning trading post he gave no hint.

Harvey sighed with relief. But then Hellfire's gaze fell upon Mollie.

The girl cowered back to press herself into Leah's skirts.

'Stay away from her,' Leah snapped, placing a hand before her child.

'I won't hurt my favourite little girl.' Hellfire hunkered down beside Mollie and patted her shoulder. 'I just want to keep her amused.'

'I'm too tired,' Mollie murmured, knuckling her eyes and flinching away from Hellfire's touch.

'Even to play with me?'

'Yeah.'

'Then wake up,' Hellfire snapped, his eyes blazing. Then he softened his expression. 'Won't you?'

She cringed. 'Don't want to.'

'You ain't scared of me, are you?'

Mollie pouted. 'A little, I guess.'

'There's no reason for that.'

'There's every reason,' Leah snapped, glaring up at Hellfire. 'You killed her baby sister.'

'I didn't!' Hellfire snapped, flinching back, then pointing at the marshal. 'I didn't want to harm anyone but that man double-crossed me.'

He rolled back on to his haunches then stood and paced back and forth, walking to the back exit, then swirling round and pacing back to the door and turning.

As he reached the far extent of one of his passages, Leah shuffled closer to her husband.

'Do you really reckon this man will free us?' she asked.

Cooper watched Hellfire through one paced tour of the saloon.

'I hope so. But whatever happens, I'll do whatever I have to do to get us out of this.'

'I don't care about us, just Mollie.' Leah snuffled and lowered her head.

Cooper shuffled closer to her and placed a consoling hand on her back, but further along the bar this comment ground into Harvey's thoughts. He wanted to find a way to redeem himself. As he looked at the bar and heard Hellfire's footfalls stomp across the saloon's rotted timbers, an idea came to him.

He shuffled along the side of the bar to sit beside Leah.

'I have an idea,' he whispered from the corner of his mouth while watching Hellfire pace. 'If you're only bothered about getting Mollie to safety.'

'Then do it,' Leah snapped.

'Leah!' Cooper muttered, his comment forcing Burl to glance his way, but as Hellfire was still pacing back and forth, he quickly returned his gaze to him.

'I don't care if I die,' she whispered, 'as long as Mollie lives.'

'And what kind of life will that be for her?'

Leah frowned as she considered this comment, but Harvey laid a hand on Leah's arm.

'A good one,' he said. 'Both my parents died when I was young, but Shelton Baez brought me up well and I've enjoyed my life – until now.'

'You heard him,' she said, looking up at Cooper. 'If he can get her to safety, we have to help him.'

Cooper shook his head. 'I won't do—'

'Be quiet,' Burl muttered pacing up to them. 'You're all talking too much.'

Leah snorted and rolled to her feet. She faced up to Burl then slapped his cheek.

Burl grunted and moved to grab her hand, but she bunched her fist and slugged him in the guts. The blow landed without much force, but it caught Burl unawares and he staggered back and fell to the floor.

Hellfire's men roared with laughter, that sound redoubling as Leah leapt on Burl and slapped his cheek, then lunged for his hair. She gathered a good grip and began a steady pounding of his head on the floor.

Harvey stared in open-mouthed shock, but Leah broke off from her fighting to glance at him, then

128

at Mollie, and Harvey realized she had acted so foolishly to give him a distraction.

So, with everyone watching the fight, he took Mollie's hand and led the sleepy girl behind the bar.

Hellfire's men taunted Burl about his poor fighting ability. But then Burl gathered his wits about him. He grabbed Leah's wrists and pushed her up and away from him as he regained his feet.

Harvey took this as his cue and slipped under the bar. The hole through the floor to the under-side of the saloon was there and he pushed Mollie into its inky darkness, then jumped down after her.

Below the saloon, the three-foot space provided just enough room to wriggle on his belly. With the smaller Mollie crawling along before him, they headed under the saloon and towards the road.

'You've just made a big mistake, woman,' Burl grunted, his voice a few feet above him.

'Burl,' Hellfire muttered, 'you won't hurt her.'

A scuffle sounded, presumably as Burl pushed Leah to the floor. Then more shuffling sounded along with subdued muttering as everyone returned to their former positions.

'Where's the child?' Burl shouted. 'And where's the other one?'

For a moment voices babbled, then Hellfire called for silence.

'Where is she?' he roared.

'Who?' Leah said.

A long silence dragged on, giving Harvey and Mollie enough time to reach the underside of the boardwalk. Then Hellfire roared with anger.

'Find them!'

Harvey continued his steady progress along the underside of the boardwalk, then peered out into the road. His foreshortened view of the road let him see the cage and the boots of a line of men as they hurried off the boardwalk and out into the road.

At his side, Mollie whimpered, so he placed a hand over her mouth.

'Can you be real quiet?' he asked.

She peered at him over the hand, then gave a slight nod.

Harvey removed his hand, then winked at her and she returned a more confident nod. With her leaning back against his shoulder, he watched Hellfire's men spread out in all directions.

Back in the saloon, raised voices questioned Leah as to where they had gone, but from the tone of Leah's response, Harvey reckoned she was still refusing to acknowledge the question.

Then a cry of triumph ripped out. He glanced over his shoulder to see the outline of a hand reaching down through the hole behind the bar.

Harvey judged that it was only a matter of moments before somebody stuck their head down and saw them. He glanced out into the road and confirmed that the men who had left the station weren't currently in the road, so he tugged Mollie's arm and they slipped out from under the boardwalk and stood.

He glanced at the cage. From inside, Lincoln

was looking their way and he pointed down the road, then over his shoulder, which Harvey took to be the directions Hellfire's men had gone. Most of them had gone to the store, the most complete of the standing buildings.

Harvey glanced left and right. Nowhere would provide them with a substantial hiding-place, but the nearest building was the station. Seeing no alternative he scurried past the saloon with his head down and led Mollie by the hand.

The station was so ruined that Hellfire's men hadn't bothered to head down to this end of town. Harvey peered around, then edged on to the ruined platform.

But then, behind him, the remainder of Hellfire's men clattered out of the saloon.

Harvey shuffled into the hulk of the station. The standing and blackened beams were just a skeleton of the former building. Even by moonlight they wouldn't provide cover from a search for more than a few seconds.

Mollie started to shiver beside him, but whether that was from the night chill or fear Harvey couldn't tell.

He sought out the least dilapidated corner of the station. Two-foot-high boards provided protection from casual sight in the moonlight and he knelt there. He drew Mollie close to him and began a silent prayer that they would be lucky.

But then his prayer grew in volume and he directed it towards the only person who could really help them.

'I know you're here,' he said. 'I need your help and I need it now.'

He waited, but no answer came.

'Hellfire will kill me and this girl,' he continued. 'She's only young and he's already killed her baby sister and she's mighty scared. We need you.'

Harvey waited, but from behind the blackened standing wall, he heard footsteps approach as Burl clattered on to the station's platform.

'Get over here and bring some light,' Burl shouted. 'I heard someone talking in the station.'

'They're going to find me,' Harvey whispered. 'And I'm betting my life and Mollie's life that you're the only one who can help us. You got to act now or we'll die. Please help us. Please.'

He glanced around the station, but all was still. By the lights from further down the road, Burl's shadow fell across the edge of the station building, lengthening as he walked closer.

Harvey gritted his teeth, knowing capture was only moments away.

'Please do something,' he murmured. 'Please.'

Two feet to his side, a trapdoor in the floor silently swung open.

CHAPTER 13

'You'll never find him,' Lincoln shouted through the bars. 'Harvey's escaped.'

'Be quiet,' Hellfire roared, aiming a firm finger at Lincoln, 'or your real suffering starts early.'

Lincoln shrugged and leaned back in the cage, but even though he kept his gaze on the guards, he glanced around Calamity from the corners of his eyes.

To have survived one encounter with Hellfire, Harvey must be a resourceful young man – even if he didn't show it when Hellfire had attacked the saloon – and he reckoned that if there were a way to help him, he'd take it. But, trapped in the cage, he saw no opportunity to do anything.

He directed taunts at Hellfire's men, hoping to distract them from their search, but they all ignored him. After they'd failed to find anyone in the station Hellfire sent men to search down the railroad tracks in both directions, but in the moonlight they found no sign of him or Mollie and soon returned.

With first light just a few hours away, Hellfire called off their search and his men returned to the saloon.

He left two men to guard Lincoln's cage. Both men paid little attention to Lincoln as they listened to the raised voices inside the saloon as Hellfire questioning Cooper.

From the lawman's scared tone Lincoln judged that it was debatable whether he would live to see Lincoln's scheduled death at sun-up.

But after fifteen minutes the raised voices petered out. Shortly after that, snoring sounded from within the saloon. By then the first arc of light was spreading across the eastern horizon. As the light grew an early-morning mist descended, pressing a cold clamminess around him.

The guards grumbled as they paraded back and forth. With increasing frequency they loitered by the fire they'd built to warm themselves. But as time passed that grumbling grew and mainly involved the failure of two other men to relieve them. They debated whether to leave Lincoln to kick that relief awake but then became silent, nudged each other, and swung round to face down the road, looking beyond Lincoln's cage.

Lincoln shuffled round to look in the same direction. He hoped that maybe Harvey had gathered the courage to try to help him, but instead he saw a caped figure emerge from the mist-shrouded gloom around the station.

As it closed on the cage, it appeared to glide as

the cape brushed away the ground mist. A cowl hid its face.

'Who in tarnation is this?' one of the guards murmured.

'It ain't Harvey.' The guard narrowed his eyes. 'I reckon it's a woman.'

'Nobody lives in Calamity.'

The other guard placed a hand to his heart.

'They don't, but I've heard that the station is haunted.'

The other man snorted. 'That ain't no ghost.'

The figure continued to glide towards them over the mist-shrouded ground.

'Hey,' he shouted, 'stay back.'

But the figure maintained its steady progress. After another five yards the man drew his gun and swung round to face it.

'Stay away or I'll shoot.'

The figure continued to advance.

'Stay back!'

He raised his gun to shoulder-level and took sight down the barrel. This time the figure halted. Seconds after it had stopped the cape rippled to stillness, but then the figure just stood there, ten yards before the guards and to the side of the cage.

'You just saved your life. Now, you can raise your hands and come here.' The guard stood poised, waiting for the figure to move, but it didn't move. 'You heard me. Come now or die where you stand.'

The figure didn't acknowledge the threat but continued to stand exactly where it was.

Lincoln shuffled to the front of the cage and

peered at the figure, hoping to see who it was, but the cowl shrouded its face.

'I said,' the guard continued, 'come here.'

The figure was like a statue.

The other guard paced forward.

'I've had enough of this,' he grunted.

He stomped to the figure's side and hurled back its cowl, but then staggered back a pace, a pained screech escaping his lips.

With a swift gesture, the figure replaced the cowl before Lincoln could see who it was, but the man still staggered away, his body bent double.

As he staggered round on the spot, Lincoln saw that his hands framed a knife, which protruded from his chest, the blood gushing over his hands suggesting that whether or not he removed it the blow was fatal.

The other guard stood rigid, his mouth open with silent horror. When the second guard had staggered round in a circle the figure darted forward, whipped the knife from his chest, and advanced.

As if this movement broke the first guard from his torpor, he raised his gun, but as he firmed his hand, the figure hurled the knife. The knife flew through the air and hit with deadly accuracy, transfixing his neck.

The gun fell from the man's slack fingers unfired. His hands shot up to his neck but the torrent of blood cascading over his hands let him do nothing more than utter a pained bleat before he keeled over to sprawl over the other guard.

The figure merely glided towards him and removed the knife. It wiped the blade on the man's jacket, then knelt beside him, removed his key, and shuffled towards the cage.

With its head lowered, the figure unlocked the cage and stood back.

'Obliged,' Lincoln said. He walked his hands up the cage bars until he was standing, suppressing a wince when his many bruises announced their discomfort, then he staggered into the doorway and stepped outside.

Without looking at Lincoln, the caped figure turned and headed down the road towards the station.

Lincoln glanced at the saloon. He could only hear snoring from Hellfire's men inside, the subdued screams of the guards not having alerted them.

He collected the guns from the dead men, then staggered round to face the saloon, but after his prolonged beating even standing was painful, never mind the full-on assault he'd need to free Leah and Cooper.

He glanced at the figure, hoping for more help, but now it was closing on the station. On the edge of the platform the figure stopped to glance at Lincoln, then continued.

Lincoln shrugged, then followed it to the station.

'Lincoln's escaped,' Hellfire roared as he stomped to a halt in the saloon doorway. He fixed his wide-eyed glare on Leah. 'And that means you're going in the cage.'

Hellfire stormed across the saloon towards Leah. Cooper jumped up to block his way, but with a back-handed swipe Hellfire batted him to the floor and grabbed her arm.

'Don't,' Leah whined, tearing herself away, then backing until she slammed into the wall. 'That had nothing to do with me.'

'And I reckon it did. You helped Harvey to escape.' Hellfire swirled round on the spot then hurled his hands aloft. 'Torch everything. Burn Calamity to the ground.'

Hellfire's men stood a moment, then ran out into the road and used the fire to light brands. As they scurried from building to building, Hellfire dragged Leah out into the road. She struggled, but he had a firm grip of her arm. He walked her across the road and to the cage.

She threw up a leg and planted it beside the cage door, but Hellfire kicked it away, then hurled her into the cage. She swirled round and threw herself at the door, but already Hellfire was slamming it shut.

Burl dragged Cooper out into the road. As soon as he was outside two other men hurled brands into the saloon. Within moments flames were licking at the walls.

Then Burl threw Cooper to the ground in front of the cage.

'Do you still say you don't know what happened here?' Hellfire demanded, kicking Cooper towards the cage.

Cooper rolled to a halt. He glanced into the cage at Leah, then shuffled round to face Hellfire.

'I got no idea what's happened to Harvey and Mollie. And I got no idea what's happened to Lincoln.'

'Tell me where they are, or I torch this pyre and you can watch your woman go up in flames just like I watched my woman burn.'

'I can't answer your question,' Cooper murmured, lowering his head, 'I just can't.'

Hellfire snorted and swaggered past him to stand in the centre of the road.

'Lincoln,' he roared, his voice echoing down the flaming road, 'you got ten minutes. Then this woman dies with Calamity.'

Around him, Calamity burned.

The long, hot summer had made the buildings tinder-dry. Within minutes every building was alight and flames rippled into the dawn sky to greet the start of a new day.

Beneath the station building, Lincoln peered at the caped figure before him, then around the hole.

The figure had led him to the station and there, beneath the rubble was where it lived. This had been an underground storeroom, but by the first hints of the lightening sky which were sprinkling around the edges of the trapdoor, Lincoln could see that this person had made a home for itself here. From the figure's slight stature, Lincoln had decided his saviour was a woman, but beyond that, he'd learnt nothing.

Crates of provisions lined the walls and in one corner stood a rusting cage, its presence hinting at the solution to an old mystery. In the opposite corner sat the subdued forms of Harvey and Mollie. Lincoln tipped his hat to Harvey and flashed a smile at Mollie, receiving timid smiles in return, then turned to the caped figure.

'You seem to have plenty here. Perhaps Shelton Baez didn't need to get any more food for you.'

The woman peered back at him, her cowl hiding her face. Lincoln waited for her to reply, but when she didn't he leaned forward and spoke again.

'Shelton gave Harvey a list of provisions. He was worried about you.'

Again Lincoln waited for a response, but again, the darkened hole of the cowl just stared back at him.

'She won't talk to me,' Harvey said. 'But she did save you and I guess that's all I asked from her.'

'And I'm obliged, but that still leaves the question of who she is. And I reckon there's only one answer.' Lincoln smiled. 'You're Adele. The woman Hellfire kidnapped, then fooled himself into believing she cared for him.'

Lincoln watched for a reaction and this time, she inclined her head an inch, but whether that was an accident or to encourage him to continue, Lincoln couldn't tell.

'You've lived here on your own for sixteen years. Some even think you're a ghost. That's a long time for anyone to keep their own company.'

This time Lincoln stayed silent, hoping that his quietness would force an answer from her. By degrees she raised her head, the first light letting him see the outline of the face beneath the cowl, if not the features.

'And over all that time, you've been Shelton Baez's best customer. So much so that he was prepared to die to keep your identity secret. You've kept him in business by paying handsomely for his help. Thousands and thousands of dollars from the money that was once in that cage.'

'It wasn't like that,' she said, speaking for the first time, her voice grating, the timbre and the slow way she intoned every word suggesting she seldom spoke.

'I can believe that. Shelton was a good man and would help anyone even if they couldn't pay. But why let everyone think you're dead?'

'Shelton knows why. Others have guessed.' She provided an odd snorting sound. 'But they pretend they don't know.'

'Why?'

She didn't reply immediately. When she did Lincoln heard the pleading in her tone for him to desist from his questioning.

'Because I want them to.'

'You have nothing to fear from me or from Harvey if that's your reasoning. I know what happened here and I know you weren't with Hellfire willingly. You won't face prison for your part in what happened.'

141

'Prison,' she grunted. She glanced around at her living-quarters which were as small as the smallest prison cell Lincoln had ever seen.

'Yeah. There's been too much suffering because of what happened here.' Lincoln provided a smile. 'Perhaps it's time for you to end your suffering.'

'My suffering will never end.'

'I have an idea of what Hellfire might have done to you in the six months before he torched this station.'

'Hellfire did nothing but care for me in his own twisted way, but sometimes we make our own hells and our own prisons.' She gave her odd snorting sound again. 'He didn't burn anything. I torched the station.'

'Why?'

'To escape.'

Lincoln winced. 'It was a good idea even if it failed.'

'It wasn't. People burned to death. And the unlucky ones survived.'

Slowly, she raised a gnarled hand from beneath her cape and grasped the edge of her cowl, then removed it and, by the faint light, Lincoln saw the true horror of what being a survivor of this burnt station meant.

Mollie screeched and buried her face into Harvey's jacket. Harvey just gulped, but Lincoln stared straight at her, meeting her eyes, the only part of her features that hadn't lost their humanity.

'Just because the fire scarred you, that ain't no

142

reason to hide away.'

'It isn't.' She ran her hand over the expanse of gnarled scar tissue that now constituted her face, then over a single tress of blonde hair, the last vestiges of what would have once been a proud mane. 'But down here, I don't have to face what Hellfire made me and he hasn't destroyed me.'

'As long as you hide, he has.'

She folded the cowl back over her face.

'Whatever you say, I can't leave.'

Lincoln nodded, but then sniffed, reckoning he detected burning. He glanced at the trapdoor. By the light emerging around the sides of the door he saw a faint plume of smoke ripple downwards.

'I reckon you ain't got a choice,' he said.

CHAPTER 14

Fire raged in Calamity again, but this time every building was alight and providing a solid wall of flames and smoke around the cage in the middle of the road.

Lincoln knelt on the side of the trapdoor, judging the extent of the damage and deciding that only the station stood a chance of surviving the inferno. He ducked down to look back in the hole and cautioned silence, then paced away from the trapdoor.

He saw that on the platform a man stood with his back to him. He was torching a heap of wood in the corner of the station, but Lincoln paced behind him then grabbed him from behind. He pulled his arm tight against his throat and held on.

The man struggled, the brand falling from his numb fingers, but Lincoln tightened his grip until the man slumped, then let him fall to the ground.

Harvey climbed out from the hole and stamped around, extinguishing the flames that had already taken hold. But when he'd put out the flames, he and Lincoln had to agree that this building was the only one they could save.

Lincoln patted Harvey's back, pointed at the hole then headed along the platform. When he didn't hear the trapdoor close behind him he turned, to see Harvey remove the gun from the supine man.

'I got me another gun,' Harvery said, hurrying to Lincoln's side.

Lincoln glanced at the weapon. 'And you'll just get yourself killed, kid. Stay with Adele and Mollie. I'll save the others.'

'I ain't no kid, and there's about ten men out there.' Harvey gulped, then stood tall and rolled his shoulders. 'When I last faced them, I did nothing, but not this time. Let me help.'

Lincoln weighed up the minor damage this young man could inflict on Hellfire's men against the greater possibility of his getting himself killed, but as he had to admit he was desperate for any advantage, he nodded.

'All right, Harvey. Head on around the outskirts of town and come at them from the opposite direction. When I start firing, take out whoever you can, then run.'

Harvey beamed with delight then ran out of town leaving Lincoln to walk down the road. The smoke swirled and eddied before him and he took a deep breath before he waded into it.

Lost within the smoke, the town crackled with insistent heat, but with each pace that he took down the road he heard a tapping that sounded above the crashing of falling timbers and the shouts of Hellfire's men. He guessed it came from someone trapped within the cage and, when the smoke cleared before him, he saw that Leah lay in the cage, beating a worried rhythm on the bars. Marshal Cooper lay sprawled beside the cage, hunched and cradling his bandaged hand as he stared down the road at Hellfire and his phalanx of men.

Lincoln paced through the last of the smoke to emerge beside the cage, his gun held down, his gait slow.

He counted ten men standing with Hellfire. With the fire razing Calamity to the ground, there was nowhere where anyone else could hide, but even so, the odds stacked against him were as impossible as anything he'd faced. Still, he stood before them while searching for a possible advantage that could keep him alive for long enough to kill Hellfire.

Then one of Hellfire's men looked his way, flinched, then shouted out a warning.

Before anyone else reacted, Lincoln swung up his gun and ripped gunfire into the men to Hellfire's right side, sending two falling to the ground clutching their chests. Then he leapt to the side to avoid a volley of returning gunfire. He kept the roll going towards the saloon, slugs blasting all around him until he came to a halt on his belly.

With his arms outstretched, he fired up, taking another man through the chest, but then the rest

146

scattered, taking positions behind whatever cover they could find.

A burning plank fell from the saloon roof, landing a yard away from Lincoln. With that encouraging the rest of the roof to collapse, he rolled the other way, then to his feet to scurry behind the cage and hunker down behind the heap of firewood.

'You all right?' he asked, glancing at Leah through the bars.

'Yeah,' Leah said. 'Is Mollie safe?'

Lincoln glanced over his shoulder at the station. 'Yeah, she's safe.'

She put a hand to her heart. 'Then you have my gratitude, whatever happens next.'

Cooper shuffled around the cage to join Lincoln, but he stared at his feet.

'You did well in that, Lincoln,' he said, his voice registering shame. 'But I still say you did wrong in endangering us.'

'And so did you. You should never have helped Hellfire.'

'I guess there's no way a man like you would understand what having your family threatened can do to your mind.'

'I know exactly what it does and that's why I have to get Hellfire.'

Cooper looked up and met Lincoln's gaze.

'I don't understand.'

'Why do you think I was so desperate to end the siege in the station the last time?' Lincoln watched Cooper shrug. 'My family lived in Calamity. They were amongst the hostages. I did everything I could to get them out, but it wasn't enough.'

'I'm sorry,' Cooper murmured, kicking at the dirt at his feet. 'I didn't know.'

'So, believe me. I know what it feels like, but you have to put it out your mind and face the likes of Hellfire head on.'

'He's right,' Leah said from the cage. 'Mollie's safe now. We got nothing else to lose.'

Cooper took a deep breath, then firmed his shoulders and peered around the side of the cage. In the centre of the road, Hellfire and two of his men were hiding behind a heap of wood. Two more men were hiding behind a mouldering buggy. Two more were behind a barrel. The body of one of the outlaws lay twenty feet away from him.

'Cover me, Lincoln,' he grunted.

'What you doing?'

'Facing the outlaws head on, like you said.'

Cooper stayed long enough to receive a nod from Lincoln, then ran down the road doubled-up.

Lincoln jumped up to fire at Hellfire's men and, from the opposite end of the road, Harvey chose that moment to help him.

Harvey's gunfire was wild, but the unexpected direction of his shooting caused one man to veer out from behind his cover. Lincoln made him pay for that mistake as Cooper skidded to a halt beside the body and tore the gun from its hand. Then he rolled behind the body and, using it as cover, laid down a burst of gunfire at Hellfire's men.

With gunfire coming from three different directions, two men were foolish enough to try to get an angle on Cooper and Harvey, but Lincoln and then Cooper tore gunfire into them that sprawled them over the buggy. But the remaining men had the sense to realize that Harvey was in no danger of inflicting damage on them and they stayed down.

And when the stable collapsed, spilling burning embers over the road near to the heap of wood Hellfire was hiding behind, Cooper scurried back to rejoin Lincoln beside the cage. With a few gestures, Cooper and Lincoln agreed that they had severely reduced the number of people they faced and that, for the first time, they stood a chance.

And Lincoln watched with delight as the remnants of the stable fell in upon itself and a flaming plank fell on to the wood heap, igniting it. Hellfire had just four men left and three of them were with him behind the heap of wood. And, as the flames took hold, the heat would force them to emerge soon.

Then one man did emerge, but when he jumped up he was clutching a burning brand which he threw towards them. It flew end over end to bury itself in the kindling below the cage.

Lincoln covered Cooper as he scurried out from the cage and kicked it away, but he wasn't quick enough and the low wind whipped the flames into life. Within seconds, a fire had shot up around the base of the cage.

Inside, Leah screeched and backed into the far corner away from the flames. Lincoln and Cooper grabbed the bars and tried to yank the cage away from the pyre. But it was heavy and whenever they managed to put any pressure on it, Hellfire peppered them with gunfire and forced them to desist.

'I have the key,' Hellfire shouted. 'Hand Lincoln Hawk over, Cooper, and I'll let you have it.'

Cooper shot a pained glance into the cage at Leah, but then gritted his teeth.

'I'll see you in hell,' Cooper shouted, 'before I hand over a fellow lawman.'

Hellfire laughed. 'Leah will get there first.'

'No she won't,' a croaked voice said from behind Lincoln. 'You only wanted that money and I have it.'

Lincoln glanced over his shoulder to see that Adele had emerged from the swirling smoke and was heading down the road. Her cowl was still over her head, but in her hand was a bulging bag, the weight great enough to make her stumble as she paced through the smoke, heading straight for Hellfire.

A smaller shape was shuffling along behind, but Adele was aware that Mollie was following her. She glanced back and signified that the child should stop, then she continued down the road.

As Mollie slumped to sit cross-legged on the ground, Hellfire and his remaining outlaws edged out from their cover to watch Adele glide down the road.

'Who are you?' Hellfire shouted.

'You know who I am,' she croaked, 'Jeremiah Court.'

Adele walked past the cage and continued down the centre of the road towards Hellfire, who stared at her, his mouth open. The other outlaws covered him, but Hellfire was oblivious to them as he stared at the approaching figure.

'Nobody calls me by that name no more. Who are you?'

'You know me,' she said.

'Adele,' he murmured, a huge smile softening his blemished features, 'I knew you were alive. I knew.'

'I may not be alive.' She stopped twenty feet before the burning heap of wood and dropped the bag at her feet. 'But I survived.'

'Have you returned to me?'

'No. I'm just here to give you what you really wanted.' She kicked the bag over, the open top spilling a flurry of bills to the ground. The breeze fluttered several bills away for them to fly into the flames and burn.

Hellfire's men boggled at the money, but Hellfire never moved his gaze away from her.

'You got it wrong, Adele. I never wanted anything but you. I did it all for you, everything.'

Adele uttered her odd snorting sound through the ruined mass of tissue that was her nose, then reached up to remove the cowl from her head. The men around Hellfire staggered back a pace, their lips curling with distaste, but Hellfire just smiled.

151

'You're just as beautiful as I remember,' he said, pacing towards her.

'And you're just as deluded as I remember.'

'Only when I'm with you.'

He stopped before Adele and looked her up and down, still smiling, then reached out to finger the ridged edges of her scarred cheeks. Adele flinched back, then reached down to the bag and raised it.

'You don't want this money?' She held it to the side, closer to the flames, more bills spilling out to catch stray sparks and burn.

Behind Hellfire, his men glanced at each other, gulping.

'I don't want that. I just want you.'

She nodded then slipped her other hand into her cloak. When it emerged, she clutched her knife.

'Watch out!' Burl cried, breaking into a run.

Hellfire raised a hand, his eyes never leaving hers to look at the knife.

'My woman would never harm me.'

Adele lunged, the point of the knife brushing Hellfire's chest, but Burl tore gunfire into her, the slugs ripping into her chest and knocking her back for her to crash to the ground. The bag flew from her hand to land on the very edge of the flames.

'Adele!' Hellfire cried, staring down at her writhing form. Then he swung round and peppered lead at Burl and the other men.

Burl flew backwards, his chest holed. The others ran for the bag. Hellfire killed two before they'd managed a single pace. As the last man threw himself to the ground Hellfire fired down at him. The man slid to a halt with his fingers just inches from the bag before he bit the dirt.

Then Hellfire hurled his gun away and fell to his knees to cradle Adele in his arms.

From beside the cage Lincoln ran his gaze over the scene, seeing that in his grief Hellfire had eliminated everyone; the only danger now came from his own grief-torn form and the burning pyre.

'Hellfire,' Lincoln roared, 'the key.'

Hellfire stood in the centre of the road with the dying Adele cradled and sprawled backwards over his arm.

'Give it to him,' Adele murmured, her voice pained and fading, 'and we can be together.'

Hellfire gave a frantic nod, then rummaged through his pockets. He found the key and held it out, but it fell from his trembling fingers.

While Lincoln covered him Cooper broke into a run, then threw himself to the ground, sliding over the dirt as he grabbed the key. Then he hurled it over his shoulder to Lincoln, who swirled round and ran back to the cage.

He leapt through the flames to grab the door, then thrust the key in the lock and hurled open the door.

Leah leapt through the advancing flames, tumbling over Lincoln in her haste to escape. As they rolled clear of the cage Cooper joined them. He hugged her a moment, but when they stood it was to see that aside from the bodies and the sprawled form of Adele, the road was deserted.

But then Lincoln saw movement as Hellfire picked a route past the burning debris of the collapsed roof to enter the saloon. He would have let him go to meet his death in whichever way he chose, but thrust under one arm was the small shape of Mollie.

Cooper moved to follow him, but Lincoln grabbed his arm, then signified that he should stay and keep Leah safe. Then he hurried across the road, tearing his jacket from his back so that he had something to throw over his face and protect himself from the flames. Even so, he had to leap through a growing wall of flame to enter the saloon.

As he hurled the flaming jacket away from him, he saw that Hellfire stood in the centre of the saloon, the flames rippling around him, the child in his arms.

'You ready to kill an unarmed man, Lincoln?' he asked.

'I will if I have to, but put down the child. This is about you and me. Like I told you it always would be.'

'I know that, but you got a weakness, Lincoln. You care about people.'

'I do. But so do you. I saw what you did for Adele.' Lincoln raised his gun and, standing sideways, aimed at Hellfire's head.

'And now it all means nothing. You may think of killing me, Lincoln.' Hellfire rocked up on his heels then down, the action shaking the rapidly weakening floor. 'But when I die, I will fall through this floor and I will drop this child into the flames. And that'll be enough to stop you firing.'

'It will stop him,' a voice said from behind Lincoln, 'but not me.'

Lincoln glanced to the side to see that Harvey had braved the flames to join him.

'Get out of here, Harvey,' Lincoln snapped.

Harvey ignored his demand as he edged around the collapsed and burning bar to stand before Hellfire. He held his hands wide.

'Kill me, not her.'

'Why?' Hellfire demanded.

'Because I should have died sixteen years ago,' Harvey grunted.

'You survived the station fire, too?'

'No. I wasn't even born then, but my mother did and she lived long enough to give birth to me.'

'Nobody survived that fire but . . .' Hellfire shook himself, staring hard at Harvey. 'Are you saying. . . ?'

'I'm not saying nothing other than I don't fear you no more and I don't need no ghosts to help me.' He took a long pace towards Hellfire. 'Put her down for no other reason than I asked you to.'

Hellfire looked at Harvey. His blemished face softened. He removed a locket from his neck and looped it over Mollie's head, then patted her on the top of her head and placed her on the floor at his feet. But the moment his hands left her, Lincoln fired a single shot that slammed right between Hellfire's eyes.

Hellfire hurtled backwards, landing on his back and crashing through the burning boards. Lincoln had fired at the earliest possible moment and Mollie teetered on the edge of the hole, her arms wheeling as she fought for balance.

But as a burst of flame erupted from the hole, Harvey was at her side, scooping her into his arms. He stayed just long enough to glance down into the fiery hole into which Hellfire had plummeted, then he crawled back towards Lincoln, who held out a hand to help him to his feet.

'Come on,' Lincoln said, looking all around him at the burning saloon. 'Just because he's staying in hell, it doesn't mean we have to.'

CHAPTER 15

Lincoln and Harvey picked their way outside to find that Leah and Marshal Cooper were standing before the saloon.

Leah took Mollie in her arms and while the family enjoyed being reunited, Lincoln headed across the road to save the bag of money. It was no longer there.

But unlike last time, this time he saw its fate – a smouldering heap of paper. The stable fire had grown to consume the bag and although he judged that if he braved the flames again, he might be able to save some of the money, he turned away.

In the centre of the road, Harvey had hunkered down beside Adele. Lincoln joined him to roll her on to her back then look her over, but thick blood coated her cape and it was still spreading.

'How bad?' she murmured through scarred lips.

'It's not looking good,' Lincoln said, hunkering down beside Harvey.

'Then take me back to the station. It didn't burn and it's sun-up soon.'

157

Lincoln nodded and moved to help her stand, but Harvey brushed Lincoln away.

'No,' he said, looking down at her. 'You've spent sixteen years hiding under that station. You should see the sun come up with me this time.'

She gave a weak shake of the head, but Harvey ignored her request and drew her round to face eastwards. With Harvey cradling her against his chest, she murmured another request to Lincoln to take her back to the station, but he ignored her plea and stood back.

And together, Harvey and Adele watched the sun rise, but at what point she stopped watching, Lincoln didn't notice.

As Calamity's flames began to die, Lincoln rejoined him.

'Is she. . . ?'

'Yeah,' Harvey said.

'Then you were good to her at the end.'

'I was hoping she might be my mother and maybe . . .' Harvey looked towards the saloon.

The things that Harvey had said to Hellfire had confused Lincoln at the time and the reason Hellfire had obeyed Harvey's request to put Mollie down had confused him even more. Then, he was just pleased that Harvey had found a distraction that enabled them to save Mollie, but now he saw a hint of what Harvey had meant.

And perhaps it was an idea that could tear a man apart if he considered it too deeply.

He shook his head. 'It's unlikely, but at least it was a big enough possibility to surprise Hellfire.'

'Perhaps. I've seen her often in my life, standing on the ridge and watching over the trading post, almost as if she was looking out for me.'

Lincoln glanced at the saloon, sighing.

'Do you want to believe in that or do you want to know the truth?'

'The truth.'

'Then I'll tell you. Your mother died sixteen years ago. I saw her die. Adele was no kin of yours.' Lincoln fixed Harvey with his firm gaze and he was pleased to see him nod.

'Then who was my mother?'

'I'm sorry. I can't remember her name.'

Harvey patted Adele's shoulder. 'And you don't know who this woman was?'

'I don't, but she was somebody's wife or somebody's mother or somebody's daughter, or maybe she was just everyone that died here.' Lincoln sighed. 'But I do know that Shelton Baez was your father.'

'I always suspected he was.'

'And for some reason, he didn't want you to know who your mother was. Even if I knew her name, I'd respect that.' Lincoln forced a smile. 'Perhaps if you were to ask him now, he might tell you.'

Harvey flashed a smile. 'You think he might still be alive?'

'Let's hope he is or we'll all have even more grieving to do.'

Harvey laid Adele's body on her back and stood.

'Then come on. I got to find him.'

Lincoln glanced at the reunited Cooper family, then looked beyond the smouldering and burnt-out remains of Calamity. The town had finally died today and there was nothing left here for any of them.

So Lincoln picked up the body of the woman whom Hellfire had kidnapped and kept prisoner for six months, a woman who had been pregnant during the station fire, a woman who had survived and lived on for another sixteen years.

As gently as he could, he laid her over a spare horse.

Then with the others he headed out of Calamity and, just as he'd done sixteen years ago, he rode down the side of the railroad tracks in search of what a new day would bring him.